Delfina
A Grown-Up Fairytale

Jo Priestley

The Women of Old Yorkshire Collection

What readers said:

Other titles in the Women of Old Yorkshire collection:

Acknowledgements

This is a love letter to my many grown daughters and to all young people who, much like me, will inevitably make mistakes in their lives. To err is human after all, but it's what we do afterwards in trying to make amends that counts and really shows our mettle.

Thank you again to Andrew for continuing his enthusiasm for editing with this, my fifth book, and to Megan for adapting the cover from the artwork by the artist Alana Jordan.

Thank you to (in alphabetical order) Ann, Janet, Sue and Tracey, my reviewers who have made me strive to be the best possible author I can be.

As for the book, adults are no different to children—we all need a little fairytale magic in our lives from time to time.

Chapter 1

Seven days of watching. Seven long, uncomfortable days of being on the cusp of something. Poised and ready, but ready for what, I wonder.

Shivering, this old coat which isn't mine is useless protection from the elements. My hands and feet are numb beyond feeling, the pain now a distant memory. I should not be here, but the shame I risk in being discovered is still not sufficient to drive me away.

Yesterday I thought she saw me. She stopped mid-task and turned my way, her expression hidden in shadow. I was mindful not to move, not even instinctively, to duck my head further below the branches to avoid exposure. She stared so long, pin pricks of hot perspiration tingled on my cold back.

Each day has brought a change in her. Subtle changes which would go unnoticed by someone else; someone less fixated, someone who isn't studying every movement, every nuance.

She leaves the cottage often but never ventures into civilisation.

The chimney has coughed smoke every second I've been on watch, the fire inside devouring fuel and forcing her outdoors for more kindling.

She has no choice but to leave her refuge, but I can see it's becoming harder by the day for her to gather life's essentials. She seems in pain, but I'm unsure if the pain is mental or physical, or even both. I want to help her, but it would not help me to reveal myself. She may send me away and then I can no longer watch her.

Oh, and how I must watch her.

I think back to the day I found her. The combination of snow at Christmas had left the village deserted. I imagined everyone indoors snug by their firesides and in the fold of people they hold dear.

I'm grateful for my four walls and sound roof, but that place is not my home, my place to feel festive even. I wonder if I've ever had the inclination to be festive. Perhaps once.

Sitting in that house, my thoughts were a frenzied knot; they pushed me out the door and away from pitiful looks and the bitter-sweet intrusion of people once too often enquiring after my welfare. I had exhausted my stock of platitudes.

Walking past the houses, I was a living ghost, unnoticed by villagers too busy with the pressing business of celebration.

I saw a person. The shock at the sight of another human life made me stop in my tracks and I hung back to see where they could be heading in such conditions.

The woman's gait betrayed her age. Her head wrapped in a non-descript scarf was hanging slightly lower than her back, which stooped and her movement was slow, each step drawn out and laboured in the snow. Her moss green coat hung past the top of her derry boots, and a basket dangled from her hand.

The woman turned left and suddenly disappeared. I stopped, then began carefully placing my feet in the footprints of the woman until they ended at the pavement. It had suddenly become important to cover my tracks.

I stood perplexed. I could see no gate, no distinct driveway, just the mere suggestion of a gap in the overgrown copper beech hedge. Beyond the gap was only the outline of a footpath winding out of sight. The world on the far side of the hedge was secret. My heart pounding, I had to find out where the woman was going.

I protected my stomach with my hands and stepped sideways through the narrow void. I watched and waited. Nobody appeared to challenge me, but I remained still, eyes darting in all directions. I was unable to continue onward until I was satisfied it was safe.

Eventually and with darkness steadily descending, I stepped along the downhill path, the whole time fearful of being caught in the act. Spotting the start of woodland ahead, I was thankful to find some camouflage. My muscles relaxed a little, my short breaths lengthening.

I knew I should have gone back, that I was being reckless. But something pushed me onward. I felt small in a vast, silent world.

As I emerged from a copse of hazel, I smelled the smoke of the fire long before I saw the old, tired cottage nestled in the trees. The once whitewashed building was made blueish by the fading light and though my view was interrupted by the branches, I could see enough. I watched the strangers in the flickering light cast by a single lantern in the window. The old woman had her hand to the face of another woman, who covered the hand with her own. Witnessing such an intimate moment made my cheeks burn. If they weren't a family, their bond was clearly one of love. The orange glow of the room surrounded them, the window framing the enchanting scene being played out only for me.

The room seemed to brim with life, a contrast to my still surroundings; even the air sat quietly. I should have done the right thing, I should have turned on my heel and beat a hasty retreat up the hill, re-tracing my footprints as I went, to avoid detection. But I couldn't move. I was rooted to the spot, goosebumps crawling my body.

The sound of the stream babbling in the distance broke the spell and was as comforting as the sight of the cottage. I felt suddenly safe, a sense of calm wrapping around me like a warm cloak. I decided then to return the next day. The bitter cold and snow would be a small price to pay for such a sensation.

I turned and headed back up the path, the lack of light and slippery ground a hindrance I could ill afford in my condition. I heaved and puffed my way back to the hushed lane, stopping to lean against a wall for a moment to recover. How satisfying it felt to accomplish my unexpected mission.

As I predicted that night, I've now made the same journey these last six days and once again I am here at the cottage, waiting in the shadows. The lantern has been burning at the window since mid-afternoon on this bleak New Year's Eve, but I am powerless to leave.

How much longer should I stay, I wonder? I don't want to go home, but my quandary is settled when a noise cuts through my thoughts. I catch my breath as the latch lifts on the cottage door, the inky black night heightening my other senses, so the latch sounds far louder than usual. I see a raven descend suddenly on to the roof, flapping its wings and scrawking its chilling greeting at me.

Startled, I sit perfectly still as I wait to see what could be drawing the old woman from the warmth and safety of the cottage on this occasion. Surely this will be her last venture outside today.

She stands in the dim light of the doorway as she fastens her coat to the wind and ties a scarf around her head, knotting it twice under her chin. She shuts the door behind her before heading down the path, and I bob my head lower in panic as she draws ever nearer.

She halts at the end of the path and rests a hand on the gate, the back of her scarf flapping manically to the side of her head. I can only imagine her peering into the woods because the darkness hides her features. Holding my breath, I watch and wait once more.

A powerful gust of ice wind bites me. I watch the woman raise her hand at the elbow, palm inwards, finger pointing to the half-moon. I see the silhouette of her forefinger crook three rhythmical times, beckoning me towards her.

Covering my mouth quickly with my hand, I still fail to stop a horrified gasp from escaping.

No matter. It is lost forever in the sound of the storm.

Chapter 2

It is too late to run now and know I must go inside that cottage come what may. How strange I can have such trepidation of this small, frail old woman. I can only be wary of her in a spiritual sense, not physical, but this reasoning does little to settle my nerves.

She raises her hoarse voice above the howl of the wind.

"Come now, come inside. You have nothing to fear from me."

The taut muscles of my stomach relax a little with her reassurance, my baby adjusting to the movement, settling themselves again.

The woman's voice is raspy and weakened from age, and yet there is something else. My curiosity makes me stand awkwardly in the snow, stiffened by lack of movement and the freezing temperature. I'm afraid to take this step toward the unknown, to leave my place of safety. I turn my head to look at the flattened leaves where I sat on the ground only seconds ago.

But I must leave it all behind. Sighing, I set off in the direction of my muse. She seems so familiar, yet I know so little about her other than what I have observed this past week.

I approach the wind-battered wooden gate, expecting the woman to wait for me to reach her, but she swiftly turns to head back down the path. I'm shocked at the sureness of her movement after witnessing her slow, steady decline over the last seven days.

I hesitate briefly, then follow like a loyal dog on the heels of her beloved mistress, a trust forming a crust over my fears. She tells me I have nothing to fear, and somehow, I believe her.

At the door she presses the outer latch twice with her thumb, resistance from rust delaying our entry briefly. I watch as white snowflakes disappear for good into the black wool of her coat.

She leaves the door ajar, an unspoken invitation to enter her home, and as I do, I pause to soak up the detail. Until now, I could only imagine how the cottage would be. I look down at the worn stone flags of the floor, uneven in texture and colour, neither pristine nor dirty. My eyes roam to two chairs by the fireplace, one winged and one straight-backed, then to a simple wooden dresser filled with books on the opposite wall. The room is small but adequate.

The wind yells at me now to enter and the gust pushes me across the threshold as though enraged by my hesitation.

"Come, sit by the fire to warm," she says, in her croaking voice. She heads to fill the iron kettle without removing her damp coat.

I step into her world. Her life is everywhere, washing over me, enticing me, giving me solace even. The warmth of the room hurts my cold bones as I battle to close the door to the storm, which has suddenly whipped itself into a frenzy. After a final push, I succeed, and she points to the peg at the back of the door. I remove and hang my coat, then await further instructions from my host. She asks me to sit down but doesn't indicate where, so I decide on the winged chair almost immediately. Alongside the straight chair I can see the obvious signs of a person's comfort, glasses perched on a side table, an open book, sagging cushions, threadbare arms. This chair is not mine to choose.

Perching on the chair opposite with my back to the rattling door, I watch as the woman places the kettle on the fire, its dancing flames abruptly subdued. She removes her own coat, hanging it alongside mine.

This is a home from another time, but a home in the truest sense, a nest.

I make a careful, mental note of every detail of the room as she prepares our tea, not wanting ever to forget it.

The atmosphere holds me in a warm embrace, and I would like to snuggle into it, but now is not the time to lower my guard.

I wanted to see inside, I wanted to be inside…and now here I am. I've pictured this scene for seven days, but I could never have imagined how it would make me feel if it had been seven centuries.

I drop my head and close my eyes, attempting to quash a sensation so overwhelming it threatens to crack my composure.

I hear her pour the water into the cups and know she will soon join me by the fireside. My lower lip sits between my teeth as she approaches. A teacup is placed on a table by my side, but no milk or sugar are offered. By the look of the leafy broth, it's an infusion of herbs. Beggars cannot be choosers, I think, and it's hot and therefore welcome. A hunk of bread and jam, no butter, is handed to me on a plate patterned with fading flowers that are almost washed away. I take a bite only after she nods her encouragement and then swig this down with the tea, hurriedly taking another bite to disguise the bitter flavour. My hunger and thirst subside a little; I'm revived, if not restored.

Air wafts my face as she turns to sit in her chair. She adjusts position to match the indent in the well-worn cushion, then stares into the fire. I watch her face aglow in profile. If I could speak, I would have no words. I have no need of any.

I wonder if the villagers think of her as a reclusive old witch; the witch who lives in the cottage in the woods with her fire and her folklore. Perhaps they tell cautionary tales of her to their children before they sleep. Her shoddy appearance is enough to ward away strangers, making it easy to hide alone, invisible, and unnoticed.

Yet she is no witch. In spite of her age, she retains a mesmerising beauty which refused to disappear when youth shut its door on her. Her dour clothes do nothing to distract from her shimmering hair; a white light cascading around a face of porcelain. If there are cracks to be seen, they are hairline, barely noticeable to the eye. The waves stop and rest on her shoulders.

"Why are you here? What interest could I, an old woman, be to you?" she asks, her roundish blue eyes tilting my way.

Her question has me suddenly alert, heart thumping. I've rehearsed the answer every day whilst sitting at my watch post and thought I knew it parrot-fashion, but now I must search to find the first words.

"I…I sincerely apologise for the unexpected intrusion. I mean you no harm, but I've found myself entranced by your woodland home, finding it impossible to leave you behind in my thoughts when I leave each day. My circumstances are new to me and difficult." I pause and swallow, wondering whether to continue, but I do.

"And my mind isn't my own at present. This is the truth, and I hope you can forgive me."

Her steady gaze holds mine and I see the flames glowing in her eyes. I am a trespasser. I can offer no defence, and my cause now can only be to allay her suspicions. I follow her eyes as they drop to my stomach, my hands folded across the roundness protectively.

"You're being careless, but I'm sure you know this. Harsh weather is no good for you or your child. For the sake of you both, you must keep warm, stay sheltered. You must."

The shame returns to burn me and this time it lingers. I should not be thinking only of myself in these times. I should have my child's welfare at the core of every waking thought. That I must be reminded of this is despicable.

She takes a sip from her teacup. The sip is ladylike and demure, belying her humble appearance and surroundings, and I want to know why she has chosen this life, to live in such a way. I want to know many things.

"Will you tell me your name?" she asks.

"Delfina," I reply, adding quickly, "Effie. My mother had illusions of grandeur. A teacher told me the name was absurd and asked if I had a pet name. I told him the name my father preferred to call me, and I've been known as this ever since. It spared me ridicule at school. Strangely, my mother rarely referred to me by the name she loved … or indeed by any name at all."

I stop talking, suddenly awkward about divulging too much too soon to a stranger. I smile shyly at the realisation.

"I like the name. It sounds regal, almost majestic," she says. "Whatever your name, I'm honoured you would consider my home to be a place of refuge on such a night. I hope we can be of good company to each other, Delfina, for a while at least."

Coming from her lips, my name sounds different and not just because of the rasp of her voice. This woman is the first person to whom I've confessed my real name, as it makes me so uncomfortable. Effie is less jarring and draws less attention.

Neither of us need to hurry the conversation, we don't rush to fill the gentle pauses in our sentences. I hear the whistle of the wind above the fire's crackle. The sound is one of homeliness, cosiness, as I await the inevitability of further questioning. A good while passes, the easiness of the room and the calm aura of my companion enveloping me.

"You said your mind is not your own. Would it help your state of mind to elaborate? Of course, you don't need to if you only wish to rest awhile."

She talks as if from another time; the house is as if from another time; so are her clothes and the crude, if snug, surroundings. This woman has retreated to the necessities which are the roots of life—food, water, air, shelter—and she must have reason to do so. One thing I'm certain of at this moment: elaboration could not possibly worsen how I've been feeling during these last months. My solace is bound to this room, even to this woman, but soon I will need to return to the slog; the slog which appears each day on waking, and I have only tolerated it for the sake of my child.

I have made my decision.

"I've done a terrible thing," I state baldly, the confession contorting my features. I press a hand to my mouth and know it's too late. The words can never be swallowed.

I wait with bated breath for her reaction. Will she ask me about the terrible thing? Will she tell me she doesn't wish to know of it?

There is no reaction. If I should tell her, I know it will be at my own free will and my own pace.

My relief curdles to something else as her eyes fixed upon me. She turns her face completely in my direction in one purposeful movement. My heart begins to gallop, my head jerking backwards to protect myself from the horrifying sight, but my body is unable to follow suit. I'm pinned fast into a corner, the back of my chair a barrier to escape.

The right-hand side of her face does not match the left, a coarse knotted redness protruding from the skin which is now aglow in the firelight.

The shock is tangible. Less because of the contrast to the other side of her face and more because she has taken it upon herself to show me it unashamedly… in all its wretched glory.

I have a sudden clarity. The twisted branches in the forest of my mind have been cut free, so I can clearly see the path I must take.

I stare straight and true into her eyes as vehemently as she stares back into mine. My way ahead is beckoning, shining as bright and as clear as the corridor to heaven itself.

This woman has set me free.

Chapter 3

My mother's voice disturbs the love story I've been re-enacting in my imagination. No doubt it will be different for everyone who reads this novel, but for me, their kiss is one of passion. Torrid is the exact description used in the passage, but passionate is my interpretation. I picture him panting, his hands entwined in her hair, no thought except for each other in their minds. This is a kiss I know I must experience myself one day.

"I would be obliged if you could get your nose out of that book and fetch your father from his study. Mr Cooper is due to arrive any moment," my mother commands, her voice steadily increasing in volume as my mind floats back into the ordinariness of the front room.

She would be horrified at my description, but in comparison to my recent stay in the fictional but vivid world of Woolford Hall, the room is just that. Ordinary.

I glance up to see her bustling away towards the kitchen to check the tea tray is ready and perfectly set. I know she strives for perfection in every aspect of her life, including her appearance, her home and especially her only daughter.

I follow her obediently across the chessboard floor of the hallway and turn left as she continues straight ahead. A chair scrapes the floor as Betty stands up quickly from the table. I imagine her startled and ashamed by being caught taking a breath when I know she's been busy since half-past six this morning. My mother won't say a word, but her expression will be saying enough.

After tapping my father's door, I bob my head around to see him. His head is bent as he strains to read in the weak light of the desk lamp. I relay my mother's instruction as he looks up from his newspaper, eyes still glazed with concentration. He often discusses news and politics with my mother, especially since the war. I find their conversations quite dull, but I must always hide this fact. I feel the same way about their conversations about brewing beer.

However, I know beer is our bread and butter, and if I don't listen attentively, my mother would only accuse me of being a spoilt, entitled girl. My father, on the other hand, thinks beer is a man's business, so he's already decided that this meeting with Mr Cooper is a waste of time.

"Right you are, I'll jump to it," he says, a twinkle settling in his eye, "we must never disobey orders from the captain on this tight ship Effie, my love, must we?"

Grimacing playfully at each other, he slips on his suit jacket, running a comb through his balding hair as he walks around the desk.

I can't recall him being home so early on a weekday. Does he know the full story, I wonder, or will my mother have given him a whitewashed version of the truth to spare us the shame?

The front doorbell sounds right on cue, and I hurry back down the hallway to re-assume my position by the fire in the drawing room. It's as though we're actors rushing to our places on the stage before the curtain rises. If I wasn't so nervous, I would smile about it.

My father may not think the services of Mr Cooper are necessary, but my mother was insistent. She's waiting in her chair, fiddling, and twiddling her three strings of pearls as I sit down.

I hear him before I see him. He has a refined voice and thanks Betty for taking his coat, then he enquires after her health and of her mother. He's so genteel, yet amiable, his voice always so different from any other I've heard before. I now manage a small smile, so pleased the room has suddenly become less ordinary.

"Ah, Cooper, a pleasure to see you on this cold night. This weather's enough to freeze the brass balls. Join us, won't you?"

My father startles us by bouncing the door back and striding over to the leather couch to await the appearance of our local schoolteacher.

Somehow, I can't help myself anticipating his arrival too. My father is now unfastening his suit jacket in preparation for sitting down, and I'm distracted briefly by the realisation of how suits are so cumbersome.

My mother, her dark hair coiffed to perfection by Betty earlier today, has the usual look of disdain she has when my father is nearby. My mother and I have the same colour hair and the same hairstyle which Betty tells me is 'unusual'.

"Good grief, my mother would look a right daft so and so if she copied my hairdo," she said once, rolling her eyes and tutting when she'd come downstairs from a hairdressing session, "but then again my mother isn't desperate to cling onto her youth like yours is."

How different my life would be without Betty. Her mischievous ways add colour to my long days, and I can't hide in a book forever, as she often reminds me. If only I had more to occupy my time. One day I was so bored I offered to help Betty get through her unending list of tasks. At least we could be together while we did them, was my thinking. She was hesitant at first, then I managed to persuade her.

I found out why she was dragging her heels soon enough. When my mother saw me with a dishcloth in my hand, she looked me up and down with horror as if she'd caught me with my fingers in a till. I was sent to my room and Betty explained why she reacted in such a way when she brought me my supper.

I'm still not convinced.

Mr Cooper appears now, his eyes scuttling around the room in search of my father. I haven't thought about him in years, so I'd forgotten how handsome he is. I see my mother glancing sideways, looking him up and down again. I know she will be taking in his suit, which I notice is slightly worn.

My eyes trail after him as he greets my parents with warm respect. Then he offers his hand to me, inclining his head slightly and I lower my eyes as I let my fingers slip inside his wide palm. I worry the sudden rush of heat will be visible in my cheeks as I sit down. The room is somehow smaller and I'm still looking at the floor as he settles himself at the opposite end of the settee to my father.

"Well now, here we are. I'm grateful to you Cooper for agreeing to see us at the end of a long, hard, working day," my father says.

Mr Cooper fails to notice the veiled sarcasm as he's now running his finger around the back of his collar. Is it the temperature of the room or the formality of the situation making him hot, I wonder?

My father grumbles often enough that workers aren't prepared to graft the same as in his day; that people have grown soft. A seven-hour day with an hour for lunch in the middle will be laughable in his book.

When he now takes a long breath to start speaking again, my mother interrupts, making his eyebrows knot with irritation.

"I don't wish to delay you unnecessarily, Mr Cooper, so I'll get straight to the matter in hand. I'd like you to provide my daughter with private tutoring," she informs him. It sounds more like an instruction than a request, and my father and I exchange glances.

Mr Cooper looks between all of us in confusion, and I understand why. I've just had my eighteenth birthday and school-life should be a thing of the past. He sits up in his seat and opens, then closes his mouth before clearing his throat.

"I thank you both sincerely for thinking of me, and indeed that I would be your first choice of tutor, but I admit I'm struggling to comprehend why you should require my services. Effie, Miss Thornton-Braithwaite, has been left school these last …" he mentally calculates the number, "…four years, I believe."

My father can't stop himself jumping into the conversation and talks over my mother, who I'm sure was just about to correct Mr Cooper regarding my name. Her nostrils flare at my father's rudeness, though she doesn't say a word. That conversation with him will be put on hold until later. I've watched my parents' interaction for so long, they have been like my case study. My conclusion is that I would rather stay on the shelf forever than live unhappily with another person.

"You are correct," my father says. "But we are progressive people, Mr Cooper, and think it's time Effie, erm Delfina, started to prepare for her rightful role in the business. It will be a distraction and give her something to occupy her time."

My father appears to be presenting a united front with my mother on her decision when I know otherwise from overheard conversations. I'm a little put out by his choice of words, and so is she. 'Distraction' has implications that I must have my attention taken away from something … or someone. I close my eyes briefly to the thought; perhaps my father knows more than I think.

"What my husband is trying to say is our daughter is very bright. I've ensured that I've had a hand in her education, but she didn't apply herself as she should have done at school. I thought private education would be better, but my husband disagreed, thinking the local school would give her a better grounding."

Her voice is louder than usual and she's speaking as though I'm not in the room. I squirm, as Mr Cooper will be thinking his teaching wasn't good enough for her, but my mother doesn't realise her offence.

"I have no son," she goes on, "and Braithwaite's will belong to her one day. It would help if she had a better grasp of the basics— English, Arithmetic, even some rudimentary Chemistry—so she understands the day to day running of the business at least.

I became the owner of the brewery by default, and I was married at the time, so this was not an option for me. I would like the situation to be different for my daughter. Thankfully, we live in more enlightened times."

Oh, I can't look and listen to her hoity-toity manner any longer, only grateful now for Mr Cooper's politeness, so he doesn't respond.

My mother's expression floats away, and I wonder if she's thinking back to how she came to be the owner of Braithwaite's by default. She's referring to how her brother, my uncle, should have inherited the business, but was tragically killed in a riding accident when he was just twenty-three. He fell from a horse whilst inebriated, though I only found out about him being inebriated from my father, as she forgot to mention it.

When she eventually inherited Braithwaite's from my grandfather she was married, and in those less enlightened times, grandfather and the Board decided my father should oversee the running of the business. This still cuts my mother. She tells me she was born too early, and the male chauvinists simply brushed her aside.

Not much has changed around here, according to her. The year is 1921, yet we might still be living in Victorian England, she grumbles at every opportunity.

She often rants, telling me that since the war women have been firmly put back in their place, when if it wasn't for their efforts, the country would surely have sunk.

The brewery certainly would, she says. She's frustrated Loftus is steadily becoming a land time forgot.

I'm sure Mr Cooper will know there's more to the situation than meets the eye, or than my parents are willing to discuss. The village has been rife with rumours of the goings on with the girl at Carleton Hall, gossip blown out of proportion by the villagers. Their lives begin and end in Loftus, so any happening out of the ordinary is news, and leaning towards bad, because bad news is always far more interesting. My best friend Janet told me this to console me after the unfortunate predicament I found myself in. Her kind words were a comfort at the time.

There's a knock on the door and Betty enters the room with the tea tray. She sets it down clumsily on my mother's favourite walnut side table. As she turns my way to leave, her mouth twitches into a conspiratorial smile. Betty knows all the ins and outs of our goings on, from me mainly but she admits she enjoys the odd snoop.

"You have to get your pleasure in life somehow," she said, "especially in this mausoleum of a house."

My mother shakes her head ever so slightly at Betty as she leaves us.

"I'll be mother," she says pouring the tea from the silver teapot.

She offers Mr Cooper a cup and a lemon shortbread biscuit, which he takes, then flicks his eyes my way as he sits back in his seat. I've become brave with curiosity and stare back into the blueness, somehow unable to pull away. This is a very new and exciting game.

Janet has pointed out I've been having quite an effect on boys in recent years. I haven't let it go to my head, but I find this situation intoxicating. It doesn't seem long ago that I was an invisible child living in the shadows.

However, I give myself a sharp reminder Mr Cooper is not a boy, he is a man. He is a strikingly attractive and mature man.

Betty said she found out he was exempt from going to war because of a slight loss of hearing in one ear. I have a strange sense of relief he didn't have to go away to fight, only to return not quite the same man or not return at all. I don't understand why I would I be thinking such peculiar thoughts.

As he swirls his finger nervously around the rim of his teacup, he nods along as my father speaks as though he's in agreement, but his cheeks are reddening. He can't seem to help but glance my way occasionally when my father is distracted while I nibble my shortbread and my mother plays with her pearls. Her mind is far, far away.

I somehow have a sense Mr Cooper has arrived at a decision regarding my parents' odd request. In any case, I should imagine like me, but for other reasons, he has little choice in the matter. I suspect the extra funds from private tutoring would be very welcome for him.

My stomach is fluttering, and the sensation isn't unpleasant.

Then the sensation gives way to discomfort, and I look away quickly into the fire. Oh dear, I will never find a valid enough reason to prevent these tutoring sessions going ahead. My mother is determined, and she holds the power in this household.

Sighing, I drop my shortbread down on my plate, suddenly lacking any appetite, but I must get a hold of myself. That's if I know what's good for me, but more importantly, for him.

There is a person who I imagine waiting patiently at the schoolhouse for his return with an explanation as to why my parents unexpectedly summoned him to Carleton Hall tonight. That person would not look on favourably at him flirting with me. I'm sure they'd quite rightly consider it improper and ungallant.

The situation is confounded as the person has been lodging with Janet and her family since they came here.

The villagers have taken the newcomer under their wing and Janet says Mr Cooper's fiancé is quite the lady, with "charm in spades." I too, have spoken to her more than once and find this a very apt description.

From what I gather, she has left everyone behind to live in Loftus.

The discomfort is growing into a panic, so I don't know what to do with myself. I ask to be excused but I'm unable to wait for an answer as I would normally and try not to hurry too quickly from the room as I feel all eyes upon me.

I stand in the hallway, back to the wall, taking great gulps of cooler air.

Oh mother, you're determined to shackle Mr Cooper and me together, I know. But how could I ever tell you I'm so lost at the moment I truly hope you know what you are doing?

Chapter 4

Time has me locked in limbo. It's so much worse than boredom because I'm agitated and unable to settle, finding it impossible to focus on anything at all. Books, for once, aren't my friend because my mind only wanders away from the page.

I was determined not to give in to the temptation, avoiding eye contact until I weakened one day. Then I saw what I shouldn't want to see.

Then I decided to steer our conversations back to dull facts and figures. I wanted to do the right thing, but he wasn't on board with the plan, and I wasn't strong enough for both of us. He asked me too many questions, which somehow unravelled the fabric of my emotion which I had woven so tight and strong. After what happened before, all he had to do was gently tug at the first thread.

Now, I only have troubling thoughts of him, which I drag around like a curse. Insipid questions I cannot possibly know the answers to are so important to me. Questions such as, what time did he rise? What will he be doing or who will he be discussing?

Then there is the most pressing question of all: Is he thinking of me?

It was three distant Tuesdays ago when we were last together in this very room. In between, I've ploughed through the long festivities where my father was in trouble for having one too many whiskies at the work's fuddle on Christmas Eve. He didn't come down to join us until after midday on Christmas Day, but he told me later it was, "Well worth the lashings of tongue and cold shoulder your mother dished up."

A livelier New Year followed at Janet's where, even though I had to be home before midnight, I still managed two glasses of stout and more laughter and good, old-fashioned fun and games than I've ever had before. Betty brought the house down by doing impersonations of people from the village. These included my mother.

She sat, stout in hand, little finger tipped, pretending it was a cup of tea.

"Betty! Betty! Fetch me my pills and my magazine and my luncheon and then while you're at it, put a broom up your rear end and sweep the floor on your way up to drawing my bath to a temperature of seventy-one degrees precisely."

She used her best posh accent, and I laughed until my stomach hurt. It was by far the greatest night of my life.

Then in January and just as I thought a reunion with him was imminent, illness prevented him from returning to the tutoring sessions. Nothing too serious, my mother told me, but he thought it best not to risk my health unnecessarily.

I've missed our time together. I've missed our long, lively discussions about literature and life. My mother's timetable has been on the back burner, but I've learnt so many more valuable lessons in a few short months. Like how your body feels peculiar when you're close to someone you admire or how a smile from them is like hot sunshine. I lay in bed, reliving our time together and remember every word of our conversations.

Though I've been unable to concentrate during my sessions, I've always been far more academic than my mother gave me credit. I think she convinced herself I failed at school because she lost the battle about private education, and it doesn't sit well with her.

The days are counting down now to springtime when I start work at Braithwaite's, and I hardly dare think of it. No more tutoring, no more discussions; by spring I will be out from under my mother's feet.

My father's study is snug from the fire Betty lit earlier. The hissing of slightly damp coal burning is the only sound. It was my grandfather's study before his and there are signs of him everywhere, from photographs to memorabilia of his life. I cast my eye over the nostalgic beer bottle labels displayed in a gilt frame. I like the contrast it demonstrates between the fine and the functional and it makes me think of grandfather. I'm told he was the same. Father has the greatest respect for him because he was driven to succeed by the poverty and hunger which he experienced as a child.

"His only downfall was trying to make up for his own suffering by overindulging your mother," he told me. "She suffers from complacency, and no child of mine was going to have the same attitude. My family was poor as church mice when I was growing up, but there was always food on the table. Plain, simple fare, but nourishing, nonetheless. I never went to bed hungry like your grandfather did. That is a whole different kettle of fish. Your grandfather married your grandmother and bought this house, which at the time was almost derelict. Between them, they made it a fine family home for your mother and your uncle. But your grandmother was never the same after losing her son, and she died only fourteen short months later. This left your mother living a lonely life with her father who grew to think of nothing but Braithwaite's."

I wonder, can he not see the obvious similarities? Mother then married and began another lonely life with a husband who thought of nothing but Braithwaite's. She hasn't any friends, but Betty tells me this is because she looks down her nose at people.

Now I'm older I know the biggest problem my parents have because it's the same problem I have.

We're caught between two stools in society. We are wealthy and seen as rich and aloof by the village, but our money is new, and the landed gentry will never accept us because of it.

It's common knowledge that Lord and Lady Henstridge at the manor don't have two farthings to rub together these days and the house is crumbling around them by all accounts. However, he's a baronet and can trace his ancestors back to William the Conqueror, which means he will always be considered superior to my parents. The more they try to convince others of their standing, the less they are convinced, so they won't accept us.

Except Janet, she's the only one who accepts me completely, almost as a sister, as I do her. I've spent my best times in Janet's cosy home only a few streets away. She rarely comes here, telling me she's always on ceremony with my mother, even if she's not in the room.

"I'm waiting for the door to open any minute," she said once. "It's like she's waiting outside to pounce."

She made me laugh. Janet has shown me what a home should be like now, so I'm unable to think of the hall as homely.

"Families should fill a home with chaos and chatter and discussions about anything which pops into their minds without judgement," she said. "You'll have a home of your own one day and you'll know what to do."

I shall and I will.

Footsteps on the tiles make me catch my breath now. They're getting louder, overtaking even the sound of the rain battering the study window.

Oh, thank goodness he's here. My heartbeat falters when I hear his voice after so long, asking Betty about her festivities. She doesn't say she went home to have Christmas dinner with her mother after serving ours and preparing a cold buffet for us to enjoy in the evening. She doesn't say she was back serving breakfast first thing on Boxing Day morning as though Christmas had never happened. Instead, she tells him it was very pleasant.

She knocks and enters, announcing Edward as "Mr Cooper" ceremoniously. Betty has no idea the announcement is unnecessary, as I've been imagining this reunion in my mind for weeks now. This is the first secret I've had from her.

"Good afternoon, Miss Thornton-Braithwaite," he says, inclining his head, "I trust you are well, and you've enjoyed the Christmas break?"

"Good afternoon, Mr Cooper, I have indeed, and I trust this day finds you fully recovered."

With Betty now out of earshot, and mother having a lie down before supper, we're able to drop the pretence. After all these never-ending weeks, I'm overcome at the prospect of picking up where we left off.

"Oh, Edward, I can't tell you how happy I am to see you again. If you hadn't returned this very day, I think the sound of my own thoughts would have driven me totally mad. They've been far too loud for comfort."

I almost run from behind the desk to be near him, to hear him telling me how much he's missed our sessions or even how much he's missed me. My mind will only settle when I look into his eyes. Another power is at work, one which has made me lose all rationale and reason.

I stop dead in my tracks; his pallor is grey, and he has a strange expression about his face I haven't seen before. Something is wrong, something dreadful has happened which may stand in the way of our plans. Please don't tell me you've been absent because you're seriously ill, Edward, I think.

"What is it?" I ask, dropping my arms as though I'm already defeated.

He looks tired and drawn even in the warm lamplight, his agitation obvious.

"Come, sit down, I need to talk to you before we start … if we start," he says, nodding to the leather chairs at the far end of the room by the fire.

I set off immediately, wanting to get to the heart of the problem as quickly as possible, and then I hope we can resume where we left off.

My heart is already sinking. I somehow sense we have started in a very different place to where we finished before Christmas.

He follows close behind me, adjusting his trousers at the thigh before sitting down. I can see he needs a haircut.

His fair hair is too long, interfering with his collar. The wind has pinched his cheeks, so they stand out like the cheeks of a painted doll. He certainly looks unwell as I search his face for clues. He doesn't sit back in his chair, adding to the sense of urgency.

"I haven't had a pleasant Christmas at all, Effie and I've been avoiding my return to duty..."

Duty—what an odd choice of phrase. We're in love, we told each other this on the very last day before the Christmas break. We exchanged cards and secret gifts of a pearl encrusted broach which was his grandmothers for me, and a silk pocket handkerchief, gift boxed and embroidered with his initials for him. I had to venture to Leeds alone on the train to buy it, having quite an adventure.

"...I've been tormented with worry of the future," he says.

Ah, here it is then. Here's the sharp point of the blade waiting to cut me.

A pause makes life grind to a halt. He runs his hand through his messy hair and stands up to look out of the window as I brace myself for his next admission. It's hurtling in my direction; I can sense it. All I can do to prepare is stare at the back of him, like he's heading in another direction already.

"I can't turn my back on Susanna, Effie, she will never manage without me to provide for her.

She gave up her whole life to be here with me in this village, and she did so at my request. She hasn't done anything wrong," he lowers his head slightly, "and neither have you. The blame lies solely with me because I realise now, you're no more than a child, a beautiful, bewitching child. Please believe me when I tell you my intention was never to lead you on. I saw a wonderful future for us together at the time of my declaration of love, I truly did. I had my head in the clouds and lost sight of reality. Forgive me."

His shoulders droop telling me he's resigned himself. Tears sit at the back of my eyes, terrified already by the thought of a life without him. What can I do, say to change his mind, I wonder? I must think of something, or I may never have another chance. I must convince him our destinies were meant to entwine.

"I've read about life and love since I could hold a book in my hands, Edward, so I do know something of it. I'm aware the path of true love is blighted by potholes, by setbacks. No love worth having could be any other way. If you just slipped into it without thinking it would be meaningless."

This was how he described his relationship with Susanna. I hope now to nudge his memory so he can remember how different our love is.

He'd slipped into their courtship without giving it the thought it deserved, he said. Susanna was presented by a friend of his mother's they went to stay with as an ideal woman to plan a future with because she was single, pretty and amenable.

They chatted every day before he returned to Loftus, only meeting a few times during the year or so before she moved here. It was like slipping into a habit was how he described it if I recall.

I'm startled when he spins suddenly on his heel, then flies across the room towards me. He drops to kneel at my feet, holding onto my knees as I look down at my dress. I chose this favourite dress for our reunion, the latest trend, a little looser and a little shorter above the ankle. Betty told me the first time I wore it that the royal blue colour of the satin complimented my colouring. I chose it especially.

"You must understand, books are no reflection of real life, you'll come to know this as you grow older.

Real life requires money, tenacity, stoicism for a person to survive it. I've been foolish in thinking I could run away somewhere with you and start again. It was a pipedream. I would need to break the solemn promise I made to Susanna, leaving her to return home to her parents with her tail between her legs.

They certainly made it clear they had their doubts about me, and I'd hate to prove them right. If I left the village and the school under a cloud, I'd be unable to obtain a reference from the headmaster so how could I secure another position?

The risk is too great for Susanna, but also for you, my love. It pains me to think this, but you'll come to know I'm right in time. You'll be glad you were spared the scandal when you fall in love with a local boy and go on to have a family and be settled in your simple, straightforward marriage."

I've lost ground now as though I'm free-falling from a great height. So, he has feelings for Susanna then—I can barely bring myself to think her pretty name—I've misunderstood or perhaps I've been misled. Promises to her have never been mentioned before let alone his home, his job. Suddenly I'm a risk too far even though he told me our love would be enough to overcome any obstacle. As for scandal, I know of it already, yet I did little to deserve it. Our scandal would be for true love, nothing more, nothing less and it would peter out in time to be replaced by someone else's. This is the nature of scandals I understand now.

I look beyond the top of his head, a bud of indignation sprouting from the injustice I feel. He deceived me, I'm being cast aside as his mind is made up, I thought as much and now I know it.

Removing his hand from my knee I stand up, carefully ignoring his startled look of rejection. I retrace his steps back to the window and watch the rain bash against the panes from the storm outside.

The raindrops disperse into erratic rivulets, almost fleeing away from each other in panic.

Studying the pattern of them calms me and allows me time to consider my next move. I refuse to allow my anger to turn me into a hysterical child playing right into his hands, though my lower lip is quivering.

I don't want to wake in the morning to the dismal winter day ahead when spring seems so far away. Janet will be working in her father's bakery, and I will feel trapped here by myself.

There will be no Edward, no plan, no future. Susanna has won, she will get about her day as usual, blissfully unaware he's betrayed her. I'm sickened by this thought suddenly, for her and for me.

"I see your mind is made up," I say flatly.

My matter-of-fact tone masks my thoughts on the bleak future I now see ahead.

Only seconds later his hand touches my shoulder and I find myself leaning into the solace of it, my back relaxing into his nearness. Is there still hope after all? He pulls my shoulder gently to turn me around so he can look into my eyes. I see his need of me, and I'm unable to ignore it.

He rains gentle kisses on my face, and hope grows in my heart.

"My Effie, my beautiful girl, please don't hate me for breaking your young, tender heart. I wanted you so badly, needed you even. I felt the intensity to my bones. If only I'd met you first, I'd never yearn for another, I'm sure of it."

He does love me, it exudes from him as tears wet my face, whether mine or his I can't be sure. He's pressing his lips hard to mine and I'm responding to his longing, forgetting our terrible conversation for a moment. I could never hate you, Edward, I think.

The door springs open, jolting us apart too late when my mother bounds into the study. I should have taken note of Janet's concerns after all it seems.

"Mr Cooper, Betty has just informed me of the good news that you and your fiancée have set a date to be married! How delighted you must both …"

If looks could kill, I think it will be preferable to reliving this moment.

And if I was one of the heroines in my Victorian melodramas, I would surely swoon and crumple to the floor.

Chapter 5

Outside the cottage the howling wind ebbs and flows but never retreats.

My new confidante has her hands folded serenely in her lap, unresponsive throughout, listening intently. She doesn't rush to comment when I finish speaking, so I can only listen to the spitting and crackling of the fire as I wait for the sting of her judgement.

"You were an innocent," she concludes finally, "he was a man, one who had made a promise to someone else, and should never have given you false hope of a new life."

Her response is unexpected. I want to believe her; she will have no idea how badly. Even so, it doesn't stop me rushing to my own defence, conditioned over time.

"I regret how carried away I was by him painting such a beautiful picture of our future life together.

It was an enticing glimpse of freedom but a freedom to love far away without anyone else to cloud our happiness.

We should have known better and stopped it before it began, but I believed every word he told me. It seemed as though Edward had been sent for a reason to whisk me away, almost to save me. You may think this strange ... and silly."

I'm careful to keep my gaze straight and true into her eyes, willing them not to stray to the blazing stain on her cheek. I know why she's withdrawn from the world. How could she live each day with the stares, the whispers or worse, the recoiling expressions of strangers? She's found safe harbour here, free of intrusion into her life.

However, her social graces tell me this wasn't always the case.

"At such an age we have a certainty, if misguided," she says, "we're certain we've been equipped with the tools of life, but they're not yet fully crafted by maturity and experience. Edward swayed you by being so attentive and the lure away from what seemed an isolated life, perhaps a lonely life even. He misled you with sweet words and promises but he was not free to offer them. It would be best not to condemn yourself too harshly. Youth is a selfish beast."

I suddenly think of my mother. We never sat together in comforting stillness, we never confided our truths, explored our worries. At least, not until it was too late for me to take any direction from her wisdom.

I alter the course of my thoughts. I must.

The woman rises awkwardly from her chair to place a log on the fire. I want to ask if she needs help, but I swallow the question fearing rebuke.

She stokes the flames back to life with a thick black iron poker. Nothing in this cottage is opulent, everything is here to serve a purpose, yet it has its own utilitarian beauty. I wonder how a person can be so comfortable in such primitive conditions, but I know she has help to live here. The roof is mended, the white walls clean, she's in no fit state to see to these things herself.

"Your home is a welcome port in a storm for me, but I wonder if you find the conditions harsh to live in alone."

"You are perceptive. There was a time when I didn't find the conditions difficult at all, but lately it is a struggle. I am old."

I want to disagree out of politeness, but this would be glib. I know tonight isn't a night to waste on such things and I don't wish to waste one second of this heaven-sent opportunity.

"The rumours were unfounded," I say, after a moment, still feeling it necessary to defend my reputation, even though it was never under attack.

*

"I often wished I was like Janet. She had an easy manner around people which she inherited from her father. He was known in the village as 'The Jolly Baker'.

I only wanted to fit in. I didn't because I talked differently, dressed differently, lived in a big house. Class was very important in our village.

43

There was a certain pride in being lower class and ironically, they looked down on classes they thought above them. It seems an old-fashioned attitude now.

I doubt I'd have fared better with private education, despite my mother's thoughts on the subject. I was lacking attention at home and at school. I had Betty but my mother kept her beyond busy. She was all we could afford because mother liked to live beyond our means—father accused her of this many times over the years … and warned her.

A misunderstanding tarnished my reputation but the helpless frustration when nobody, including my own mother would listen to my explanations, is what will stay with me.

When I think of that fateful Saturday evening, I realise how naïve we were, how little we knew of the world.

My mother had given permission for me to stay over at Janet's house and how heady we were at the thought of the night of freedom stretched ahead of us.

We'd agreed to head to the Crown and Cushion in Overwood; a good hour's walk over the moor but it was where most of the locals our age went and meant less chance of our nefarious activities being reported back to mother.

"I didn't think we would be walking up and down dale for hours in this wind," Janet said, "dragged through a hedge backwards isn't the look I was going for this evening."

Our laughter rang across the moors.

"It's just as well we're heading further afield though, Janet, if my mother found out about us going to a pub, there'd be hell to pay."

"Oh, Effie, you've got to live a little, what she doesn't know won't hurt her."

The summer night was dry, and we were glad at least not to be yomping through mud in our best dresses.

"Can you keep a secret?" Janet asked suddenly, holding onto her hat against yet another gust of wind.

I nodded, my stomach tightening. Secrets are rarely good to hear.

"We're meeting some lads when we get to the pub," she said.

I stopped and shook my head.

"What lads? You are a dark horse, Janet, I didn't know you'd lured me here under false pretences."

She carried on and I followed as she jumped a narrow stream, landing in the crispy heather made brittle by the summer sunshine.

"Do you remember Larry Sutcliffe from school who was a couple of years older than us?" she asked.

I nodded. Of course, I remembered Larry.

"Well, he's coming with his friends from the mill. He asked me here tonight, and I knew you wouldn't dare come if I told you. To be honest I'm quite taken with him."

I could tell she was just by the sound of her voice. I tried to ignore my mother's disapproving expression when she popped into my mind.

"Well, far be it from me to stand in the way of true love," I said.

I tried to sound light-hearted though I was far from it. I didn't want Janet to think me a boring stick-in-the mud.

The night was so unspoilt, the mood so carefree to begin with.

"What shall we have to drink?" I asked.

"Perhaps the obvious choice … beer?" Janet said.

We knocked shoulders, smiling.

But the smiles slipped from our faces quickly when we entered the *Crown and Cushion*. We were so naïve and out of our depth in such an adult environment, with men and the odd couple cheek by jowl, huddled in a shroud of thick cigarette smoke.

I was relieved to spot Larry with his group of friends huddled to the right of the bar area. I could tell by their easy manner they were regulars.

Freddie was one of the boys, Frederick Walker who lived on Briar Street. Turning from the group he looked my way, and I remembered how everyone liked him at school.

He hesitated briefly, then smiled a wide smile and waved. I'd seen him around and about the village and knew he worked with Larry at the mill. It was either the brewery or the mill to head off to after leaving school. The pit was always the third choice for most young men around here as it was further away and harder, dirtier graft.

We'd never acknowledged each other before so his genuine smile warmed me to the core. But it also stirred something new within. I'd never been rewarded with such a smile before from the opposite sex. Until Freddie the smiles had leery connotations about them, making me feel like prey and subconsciously back away.

It wasn't just his good looks that endeared Freddie to me. He had a quietly confident air about him, never feeling the need to impress which was impressive enough in itself. His manner attracted me most however that night. He was attentive, insisting on buying Janet and I our drinks all evening. He appeared respectful and gentlemanly which are traits I've always admired in a man.

My father could be a little crude around women, and this bothered my mother and for once I could understand.

He said he was proud to call a spade a spade and didn't need to put on airs and graces to succeed in life.

I asked my mother once how she came to fall in love with my father. It was an honest enough question I thought, one which any daughter might ask but she took it as a personal affront, and now I'm older I understand why. I'd hit a nerve, and she thought I meant how *could* she fall in love with a man such as my father?

Slapping her teacup back on the saucer, she spat, "You read too much flowery nonsense for your own good, my girl. Love isn't all romantic, gushing and consuming. Love comes in all forms and sometimes people survive very well without it, you might be surprised to know.

I often think I should have made you face the realities of life instead of wrapping you in cotton wool in this house."

It was as though she'd struck me. I could never bring myself to ask my mother anything other than questions of a general nature after that day.

But Freddie was far from crude around women. He did however have a fine sense of humour, a lightness about him which was much like Janet's. Perhaps that was why I was drawn to him so much.

He threw his head back and laughed when I told him I didn't understand what all the fuss was about with beer.

"Well, I'd keep that little revelation to yourself if I was you," he said, shaking his head good-naturedly, "it doesn't look as though you're going to be the best ambassador for your brewery empire."

The taste didn't grow on me either, but Janet and I had three half-pints each over the course of about two hours. It gave me another new sensation of being slightly fuddled, the room appearing woolly around the edges.

"Come on, you look like you could do with some fresh air," Freddie said eventually, leading me gently by the elbow towards the door.

Something like anticipation, and longed-for excitement bubbled in me at the thought of having the opportunity to talk to him alone. Janet was preoccupied with Larry, and I didn't bother her on my way past because they were deep in conversation, talking animatedly. I wondered if they might have met before that night on the quiet as they looked very comfortable together. They've never left each other's side much since.

The air was cold when I stepped outside, hitting me straight in the face like a punch. Freddie's hold tightened around my arm to steady me, then he veered me around the side alleyway of the pub away from prying eyes. Although chilly, the summer evening meant broad daylight and I'm sure he didn't want to us to be the villager's entertainment for the evening.

As I leant against the cold brick wall, I struggled to focus. I tried to take in the dark curls, glued to his head with hair cream, but for a few to break free to flop alluringly onto his forehead.

His twinkling brown eyes were looking into mine, increasing the glorious wooziness I doubt was anything to do with the drink.

I thought I might swallow my own heartbeat; his nearness affected me so deeply. My night of freedom was presenting all kinds of surprises.

"So, the lady notices me at last," Freddie said, levelly, "it's only taken the best part of a lifetime."

Humour was in his eyes as he watched the realisation of his words sink in. The realisation he'd had a soft spot for me for years, all through our schooldays and beyond by the sound of it. How could it be, how could I not have seen the signs? His steady gaze upon me, I somehow couldn't look away. I was moved then by something intense, something raw.

"Why didn't you talk to me about how you felt after we left school? I've seen you around the village enough times for you to start a conversation. I have Janet now, but I needed a friend for long enough. I would have been so glad of your friendship back then, Freddie."

He closed his eyes briefly and sighed.

"How to begin such a conversation. I'm not cultured, not classy. What does a lowly mill worker like me have to offer a lady like you, Miss Thornton-Braithwaite, the beautiful girl locked in the tower of Carleton Hall?"

My throat knotted. It knotted so tightly my voice sounded different even to me.

"If you *had* spoken to me, you'd know I've no time for condescending ways. I only wanted company, somebody to be with, share my time with. I was lonely until I found Janet...or Janet found me."

His face drew ever nearer, so close I could count every one of the silky eyelashes surrounding his dark pools of love-light if I'd a mind to. But my mind was far too preoccupied.

"I don't like the thought of you being lonely," he said, "I thought you had it all. It seemed to everyone else like you did."

His lips were almost touching mine and some newfound instinct told me to shut my eyes. My breath caught.

Then a loud, lairy voice appeared from nowhere, jolting me back into the real world when I was far from ready to go back there.

"Sorry, Freddie!" Thomas Baker, one of his cronies shouted, "I just came to see where you'd got to. I didn't realise you were attending to business."

Turning on his heel he lit his cigarette behind a cupped hand then headed off with a knowing chuckle to re-join the rest of the group inside. I glanced at Freddie, expecting him to laugh too or at least dismiss the comment.

But how wrong I turned out to be.

Much like our shared moment Freddie was gone, darting with some speed in Thomas's direction. I looked on horrified as he grabbed a handful of his friend's shirt from behind as he reached him.

"I'm attending to no business, Baker," he growled, "and even if I were, it would be no business of yours."

Thomas threw his cigarette in the air and his expression changed as he shrugged Freddie off and squared up to him, jaw set, eyes narrowed to almost slits. The situation had escalated and raced off the scale in seconds.

I had never been party to such an exchange between two men, or anyone for that matter and I was stuck fast, paralysed. I shouted Freddie's name then as Thomas took a swing his way. Drink encumbered him so he was far too slow. As if in timed choreography Freddie ducked out of the way, his face contorted with fury as he then pinned Thomas firmly by his chest up against the pub wall.

"It's a bloody good job you're plastered, or I'd take great satisfaction in shutting that dirty mouth of yours. Get yourself inside, man, before I change my mind," Freddie said.

Thomas slapped Freddie's hands away, and their eyes locked in a battle-stare. I bit my lower lip watching Thomas mulling things over a second or two.

I was so relieved when Thomas did Freddie's bidding and walked away that a shudder ran through me. He threw us a hateful look as he slunk back inside without a word. How ridiculous to think now I considered it to be the end of the matter.

Freddie strode back down the alleyway towards me, his face pale and set, eyes clouded. His face changed immediately when he saw I was shaking, wrapping his arms around me, and holding me close. I sank into him, pushing my face into his chest to block out the scene replaying in my head. He smelt good …clean, comforting.

"I'm sorry it got out of hand, but I couldn't have him disrespecting you like that, Effie. I can't think what came over me. I'm not one for fighting though you might not believe me now."

He stroked my back and my turmoil ebbed steadily away until I was settled if not calmed.

"It's not how I wanted the evening to end," he whispered into my hair, "I can't imagine what you must think of me."

I didn't raise my head because I liked it being right where it was. He rested his chin on the top of my hair rocking me so gently from side to side only he and I had any idea it was happening. I was safe and I would have stayed that way forever. I wish now that I could have.

But Thomas had his revenge. He stirred the pot well, only too happy to start rumours which were twisted and bent out of shape by the time they finally reached my mother. She heard them a week later via stage whispers at the haberdashers.

I was labelled the disgraced, underage girl caught in an alleyway outside a pub whilst two millmen engaged in a fist fight over me.

It turned out to be a very long time before I had the opportunity to talk to the man who's only intention was to defend my honour."

Chapter 6

I started my new role at Braithwaite's earlier than planned when my tuition ended abruptly. The accelerated timetable was for mutual benefit; mother wanted me out of the house, and I wanted nothing more than to be out of the house and out of her way.

My shame when mother caught me in an embrace with Edward still sets my cheeks on fire. The same shame keeps me awake or in a fitful half-sleep during the night, so I can't find a moment of peace. I wake each morning knowing my mother holds me entirely to blame for the indiscretion. She says I beguiled Edward, so he had no alternative but to submit to my womanly wiles. I'd no idea I had wiles and I'm still trying to understand what they might be.

"Your fanciful ideas have yet again been your downfall," she told me, "It seems I really shouldn't have cosseted you and rest assured I shan't any longer. A silly, spoilt girl is one thing but a silly spoilt woman quite another. I can't even bring myself to look at you."

Her words scalded, leaving an indelible mark of shame inside me.

My endless apologies have only fallen on deaf ears, and my only shred of consolation is that I was the one who tried to stop us falling in love. I know I did because I sensed it was going to happen even before it did.

"How easy it is to make your mouth say anything to get you out of trouble," she said.

So, she's left me alone to fret and fester, and I have no idea how to resolve the situation. She needs me to stew in my own juices for as long as it takes, but this isn't the same as what happened with Freddie. This time I know my mother's condemnation is justified.

I may have been overindulged, I admit I've had a comfortable home, a warm bed, nice clothes, and I'm grateful for them. But there are other ways you can spoil a child, with love and affection like Janet and Betty. I know neither of them consider me coddled. Janet told me once she wouldn't have my life and all its poshness, for a gold pig.

What explanation my mother gave to my father about the hasty departure of Mr Cooper, I can only imagine. I doubt it was the whole truth because father speaks and acts the same towards me. I've watched closely for any signs of change. Thankfully, there are none; I need him as an ally more than ever.

My parents don't seem to have a relationship where they discuss the happenings of each other's day, offering each other support or a shoulder to lean on.

They think they each have a role to play in the marriage, and as part of the deal they would never want to cross the unwritten boundaries of their respective roles. My mother would never involve him in domestic matters the same way my father would never involve her in business matters.

I've found myself with plenty of time on my hands to compare their relationship to others. Janet's parents laugh and joke together all the time, they have what Janet calls banter. Once her mother was ill, and her father closed the bakery for two weeks. It caused pandemonium and I don't think the villagers, including my mother, have ever forgiven him. Betty told me someone challenged him about closing for so long and he took great pleasure in telling them he'd do it again and for longer if necessary.

"You as my customer are of course very important to me," he said, "but my wife is my life."

What could anyone possibly say to that? What a wonderful retort; jovial he may be, but I also admire him for his principles and priorities.

To have such a love. It's all I've ever dreamed of.

"Please forgive me, Mrs Thornton-Braithwaite," Edward said that terrible day, "I'm not sure what came over me. I can assure you it's the first time this has happened."

My mother shooed him down the hall and out the back door without a word at the time.

My stomach was churning as I awaited the return of my furious mother, but I could only think about the shock of discovering Edward had set a date to be married. How mistaken I was to think he was planning a life with me, when in truth he was planning a life with his bride-to-be.

The villagers are now excited about the wedding and the charming young couple who are due to set up home in the schoolhouse.

I read a passage once where the heroine described how she felt as: "Having taken a tincture of shame and regret, with just a touch of misery for good measure." I think about the passage often.

I can't possibly discuss the situation with Janet even if I had the chance. My mother confined me to the house immediately and sent her away under the pretence I was unwell.

I still feel the sting of the slap she delivered, if only in my mind.

"You, filthy little…" she searched for the word, her face puce, mouth contorted with rage, "Tramp! You will do well to keep out of my sight if you know what's good for you. What a fool I've been. My own daughter has made a fool out of me."

I cried myself to sleep and stayed in my room all the following day which is where I've spent most of my time since.

Even Betty is giving me a wide berth of late, unsure what to do or say amidst the awful atmosphere of Carleton Hall.

Father isn't home much to notice thankfully. Contrary to Janet's father, I don't recall him taking a day off work from Braithwaite's except at Christmas and then only for one day even then he worked in his study on Boxing Day as a compromise. He enjoys going to the office he told me because he doesn't consider his job to be work in the sense most people do and looks forward to the challenges it throws at him each day.

I wonder sometimes if he wishes he had a son. A son who he could proudly take into work each day to show the ropes, not an oddity of a daughter who has no need to work at all.

If he does, to his credit he never shows it. I've come to enjoy our conversations on the drive to work and look forward to our time alone.

"Well, these are strange times indeed, Effie, but I doubt the situation will carry on for long. You'll be snapped up before you know it and your working life will be a thing of the past. We can make the most of it while it lasts though, what say you?"

Snapped up, by whom I wonder. I'll wager most think me big trouble, hardly a title to win love and open doors. Time away from the big house will be just what I need.

So, Braithwaite's has unexpectedly become my sanctuary.

"Good morning, Miss Porter," I say now, taking my coat off and hanging it neatly on the wooden stand next to the office door.

I have two smart skirts, one of black and one of navy blue which I wear with a crisp white shirt each day, buttoned up to the neck with a broach. Not Edward's broach, which I have no idea what to do with as that is his family heirloom. It stared at me with condemnation each time I opened the top drawer of my armoire until I hid it.

My father has already retreated into his office which is further along the red-carpeted corridor. I imagine him striding into the arena as he calls it with a solid sense of purpose. He's a different man here to the one I know at home. But then home is my mother's domain, and he accepts this unequivocally.

Miss Porter is the only other female worker at Braithwaite's. I came to see my father during the war, and it was a different place then with only a handful of men too old to fight left behind to carry on the business, one of which included my father. The rest of the staff were women holding the fort and very well my father said, waiting for their husbands to return. Six men from our village didn't return, three from the brewery, and they will be immortalised on a new War Memorial being erected next to St Stephen's in the village. Betty's father is one of the names on the list—Joseph Dockery.

The men who did return weren't the same men who left here full of smiles and bravado. Polly Anderson's husband lost a leg, Lily Duncan's husband hasn't been seen since he re-entered the house. He has the shell shock which they say sends a man out of his mind; all have faces hollow and haunted still.

My father looked after them well. He said it was only right a hero and his family should be well provided for.

That terrible conflict touched everyone, and our remoteness was no defence. I often think how strange it must have been for the women to go back to domesticity when the men returned. After four long years of making munitions, ploughing fields, and brewing beer, suddenly they were back to washing and ironing clothes as though nothing had happened. But it had, now they had husbands who had changed, if not physically then mentally.

Betty has told me plenty of tales. She doesn't consider she has one of the worst stories to tell because she once said there are worse things than death.

"Betty, what could possibly be worse than death?" I asked.

"Well, if a person has gone, they can't suffer and if you lose someone, you suffer one emotion of loss which lessens over time. Some women have lost their man but they're still here suffering every day with no end in sight. Now that's a different kind of pain."

How wise Betty is but how much she has suffered herself to know of such things.

"Man or woman, nobody thought themselves brave," she said, "They just considered themselves to be doing what they must do. To swim until they got to the other side. So much of the quiet courage has gone unnoticed."

She spoke stoically, without a tear in her eye, but my throat was tight.

I heave a sigh at the memory. Come on now Effie, I think, if these brave people can just get on with life, then so should you.

Miss Porter is due to retire, and she plans to leave when she's brought me up to scratch with certain duties. My father told me he's been tactfully informed by certain members of the Board that the accounts are no matter for a young lady, even if she does happen to be the heiress of the brewery. They said it would be better if I concentrated on typing and the administration of the business. Having done eleven weeks of daily typing practice and shorthand, I wonder how long it will be before I'm considered ready to be cut loose.

"Good morning indeed, Effie," Miss Porter responds to my greeting, "I have some news to share when you've organised the morning refreshments."

Braithwaite's runs like clockwork, and this is due to her efforts. Miss Porter is meticulous, like an all seeing, all-knowing headmistress overseeing her pupils.

She confided that although her ailing mother needs her, she'll miss the satisfaction of working and the colleagues who have become her family. I've been given a hard act to follow, but also a valuable mentor. I'm thankful for her steady influence, especially at the moment, yet she has no idea.

I find my father deep in conversation with James Forrester when I go into his office with their tea. He calls James his right-hand man and they appear to be on the same wavelength even though they don't always agree. He was another of the men who were too old to fight so they continued to work together throughout the war.

I love my father's office. It's very tasteful, filled with leather, oak, wrought iron and whisky decanters. The only tokens of homeliness are the oil painting of my grandfather which sits over the fireplace where the fire blazes constantly.

James is the elder, and as thin as my father is round. They both have creamed hair, grey moustaches, and well-cut expensive suits in differing fabrics of dark blue, like a uniform. James's winged collar shift betrays his age, my father preferring the new fashion of a straight tie. I think of them fondly as a double act finishing each other's sentences and working in tandem.

I'm as invisible to them just as I am to my mother as I go about my work. As I place the cups and saucers on the desk, I notice again the lack of family photographs on display. James's desk in his own office is different, he has many photographs of his wife and teenage children and even one of the family dogs. They have a touch of pride about them.

Miss Porter has a cake in front of her when I return and she looks flushed, excited even. She drags her steel-coloured hair back into an immaculate bun for work and starches her collar so much it leaves a little chafe mark on her neck. She wears no embellishment, and the only softness about her is her long skirt.

"Well, Effie. I've spoken with your father, and we've agreed I will retire at the end of the month as you are now more than capable of captaining the secretarial ship," she tells me, far more animatedly than I've seen her before, "I've taken the liberty of baking a sponge cake to celebrate the start of a new era for both of us."

I raise a tight polite smile, my resolve to just get on with life waning already. Well then that's it, my fate is sealed. Now I'm on course to grow as old and as grey as Miss Porter, making endless cups of tea and typing letters until my fingers become stubs. My mother will be delighted I'm locked away in this room each day, knowing exactly where I am at all times.

I feel too queasy to enjoy the cake so kindly baked by my mentor and it sticks in great lumps at the back of my throat. I must eat it though as I haven't the heart to offend this lovely lady. I swallow hard, suddenly scared of being cast adrift, to survive here alone and under my own initiative.

Her eyes meet mine and she smiles gently.

"I know you might not feel up to the challenge, my dear, and it may seem daunting. Life is full of changes and new beginnings. I'm facing one myself and I know it won't be easy. Have faith, you too will become the backbone of Braithwaite's and over time you'll gain the experience to be strong enough to make it stand tall as I have. In time, you won't need to pretend any longer. Remember, one day you will be the person everyone looks to for guidance."

She clearly saw something in my expression I thought I had hidden well.

"Did *you* pretend?" I ask. I'm trying to be convinced as I know her words were meant to empower me, "You make it look so easy."

Her eyes twinkle warmly making the years drop away.

"Of course, how can one possibly know it all when one hasn't seen and done it all?"

Patting my hand before getting up from her chair, she smooths her already flawless hair. An unseen switch has been flicked within and she's now on course to start the first of her many daily tasks.

I pile our plates, then head to the small kitchen, thinking I must think of a way to rise to the challenge and make the best of the opportunity. The alternative of being at home will surely be the impetus I need.

"Oh, and by the way," she calls, "we have a new bookkeeper starting. There wasn't anyone suitable here to take over from Mr Bennett when he moved away at such short notice, so your father

65

decided to advertise the position in the newspaper. As it happens, he didn't need to look too far afield in the end."

I pop my head around the kitchen door and she's sitting with the silver letter opener in her hand ready to open a pile of post in front of her, delivered again like clockwork whilst I was serving tea.

"Apparently, Mr Forrester said the gentleman was doing very well at Pawson's and the fact he had been learning bookkeeping in his own time for the last two years impressed your father no end when he told him. He admires initiative as you know. I'd be grateful if you could start an employment file for him by the end of the day."

"Certainly, Miss Porter," I say, now devoid of all feeling, "may I ask the gentleman's name?"

"You may indeed. The gentleman's name is Mr Frederick Walker."

Every breath leaves my body in an instant with the shock; I can feel the blood draining from my face and swiftly return to the kitchen to hide the impact of her words.

But the shock that I would soon be working with my knight in shining armour was nothing compared to what I would later discover about prim Miss Porter.

She turned out to have many more secrets which I would never have given her credit for.

Chapter 7

My mind is not my own anymore.

As I begin to settle more comfortably in the wing chair, I think back to the vague explanation I gave my new friend as to why I was hiding in the woods, studying her for days. She should have thought me strange, but I sensed this wasn't the case. It's one of the reasons I have come to see her as a friend. I've never spoken so candidly and with such ease to any other person, not even to Janet. I readily allowed her into my confidence, and I know it is in safe hands. I have a burgeoning list in my head of things I must discuss and explore with this woman and soon.

She has replenished my drink and filled my plate with bread she toasted on the open fire using a long-handled fork. It was then buttered to plain and simple perfection. She didn't ask me if I'd like to eat some more, she intuitively knew my appetite would return once I was at ease.

I watch her still and she doesn't seem self-consciousness around me for someone who has intentionally shut herself away. I wonder for how long exactly.

Her movements are graceful and strangely mesmerising, even going about such mundane tasks and her worn wooden clogs gently tap out each step on the stone floor like a melody.

I see a door opposite and slightly to the right behind her chair. I imagine a small bedroom beyond, picturing a wooden bed, a lantern, a feather eiderdown to keep a person snug on a freezing night. A room again with purpose and functional comfort. I want to lift the latch and go inside, to rest my head as she will later. I want to fall asleep to the sound of the wind and I know I would sleep easy. The night is going on, but she shows no sign of tiredness.

"It appears you had quite an effect on your friend, Freddie," she says, smoothing her long woollen skirt, before sliding back into the cushion of her chair. Her clothes are as old and worn as her clogs, any colour long since faded and it only adds to her witch-like appearance.

"Yes, and I was astonished when I found out Freddie had secured the position of bookkeeper at Pawson's Mill. I couldn't understand how.

Over time I discovered more. It turned out he'd been going to night school for three years in his own time and from his own pocket to work towards his goal. He was working towards it even when I met him that night at the *Crown & Cushion* although the subject never came up."

"This was unusual I imagine," she says.

"Most unusual. A mill worker dies a mill worker as a rule, just as a drayman dies a drayman. They might show a bit of gumption and make foreman perhaps, but Freddie had grand plans he kept to himself.

He only let his family into his secret. It was the right thing to do, his friends would have ridiculed him if he'd told them, but he had the last laugh in the end."

Freddie had been bookkeeper for just six short months at Pawson's when the position became available at the brewery, then he spotted the advertisement. He immediately formed a connection with my father without trying. He saw him as a kindred spirit just like my grandfather had done in him years before; a self-motivated man who wanted to better himself. A man who wanted to make a success of his life.

Oh, to see his friendly face on his first morning after the long months of purgatory at home. It was so much more welcome I think as I was relieved to have someone to lean on. We didn't need to mention it would be wise to hide our former acquaintance from my father and Miss Porter.

Freddie had his own small office with only enough room to house a desk, a bookcase, and a filing cabinet. The room was a little cramped, but he called it his empire. I was oddly proud of him for achieving so much with so little; it was odd as Freddie wasn't mine to be proud of.

"Long time, no see, Effie," he whispered the first time I took his tea in to him.

He looked uncomfortable in his suit, eagerly discarding his jacket to hang around the back of his chair at the first opportunity and unfastening his cuffs to roll up his sleeves.

"I must tell you it certainly wasn't a case of 'out of sight, out of mind' these last two years," he added.

"I'm glad to hear it," I told him, smiling, and I meant it. "But you better not let Miss Porter or father see you like that," I mock-scolded.

I gestured towards the rolled-up sleeves of his shirt. As he endearingly blushed, he quickly made to roll the sleeves back down, refastening the cuffs.

Oh, Freddie, if you had been on my mind instead of Edward, I wouldn't be in the position I'm in now. I tossed the thought quickly aside as the comparison did Freddie a terrible injustice. Our paths had never crossed since that night, but then I was on a short leash.

Freddie would help to fill the void Miss Porter left very nicely indeed.

"How are you getting on as Director of Administration?"

We laughed together at the made-up title, and I told him I was enjoying my work far more than I imagined. Freddie had been forced to work his notice at the mill, so this gave me a chance to find my own routine. I was gaining confidence daily and weekends loomed far more than Mondays.

"The days fly by, I've so much to be getting on with and my father has no end of work to keep me busy. I thought I'd have the luxury of learning the ropes with Miss Porter for much longer. But now I'm my own boss for the most part, and I've found a certain level of freedom."

I stared at him then, suddenly self-conscious remembering his declaration that summer's night which seemed so long ago. How much courage it must have taken to proclaim his admiration, though Dutch courage will surely have helped. The fierce reaction to Thomas Baker's comment had convinced me of the way he felt but I can imagine he reproached himself many a time afterwards. It was an overreaction; he knew it then and he will know it now. Looking back however, rightly or wrongly he seemed to have little power over it.

He looked decidedly awkward then, his eyes floating aimlessly as he busied his hands rearranging his desk. I wondered if he was reading my thoughts. It might be best to change tack and ask him the question I'd been longing to ask for so long.

"How did you do it, Freddie, it can't have been easy finding the money to take the night classes?"

"Oh, you know, I found a few tanners in my turn-ups," he told me.

He let out a low chuckle. Was he trying to ease the tension which had grabbed a hold of us. Reliving the memory of that night was making me uncomfortable too.

"No, the truth is my grandmother left my brother and I a little pot of gold each when she died. Our Jack used his money to live the life of the lad about town for a while until the money ran out, but I had other plans. He got into my ribs for having such highfalutin ideas, but I took no notice. It would have taken more than a petty, peevish brother to throw me off course."

"I bet he really envied you," I laughed, "Jack was never going to spend his money wisely, was he? You wouldn't think you were brothers except you look like bookends."

He smiled, and I thought about his first smile when I walked into the pub that night. I basked in its warmth again, realising this hadn't happened with anyone else since. Edward was too earnest and troubled to smile at me in such a way.

"I wasn't going to waste the opportunity which came knocking on my door, particularly after our," he knitted his brows, "our conversation."

He struggled to find the correct terminology, and I understood. What a conversation it turned out to be. I remembered his arms about me in the alleyway and how it made me feel. How safe I'd been in his arms, like a child hiding behind their mother's skirts, certain they would be protected.

"What have you been up to all this time?" he asked.

How to explain this easily and to Frederick Walker. I wondered if he knew about my tarnished reputation and his unwitting part in it. If only we could have convinced people that he was only defending me and nothing more.

What have I been up to all this time? Such a throwaway question but I didn't know what to say for a second or two. In the end I said I'd been bored enough to request I work to fill my days. This was the answer which popped into my head but bending the truth to Freddie immediately felt wrong making the heat rise up the back of my blouse. His wide eyes were holding mine, showing complete trust in me.

"Can I speak frankly to you?" he asked.

I was finding it difficult to hold his gaze, anxious about what he was about to confess and how this would unfold. I silently prayed he hadn't seen through my white lie about how I came to work here. He couldn't surely know about the goings on at home with Edward, Betty would never tell, and this was the only way he could possibly find out.

He sighed, and I remembered I hadn't given him an answer. I nodded, my breath sitting in a tight ball at the back of my breastbone.

"You were my motivation, Effie. I see no point in not speaking openly or my efforts over the last years will have been pointless. I prayed the whole time you wouldn't be taken from me.

I wondered if your parents had come to some arrangement with another family about your future. The thought followed me around like a black cloud all the time we were apart. I was constantly waiting to hear news of an engagement."

He skirted around the desk and perched on the edge, just in front of where I stood. I stayed exactly where I was, there was no need to back away from Freddie.

"You drove me onwards, my desire to be good enough for you, or perhaps good enough for your family."

He watched me intently, the only sound the distant clatter of the horse's hooves and the voices of draymen outside, their words imperceptible. He was waiting for a reaction, a clue to what I thought about his admission no doubt.

My head was shaking as his words sunk in. Had I misheard? Surely, he would have moved on from me after all this time. I thought he would have found a girl and be engaged himself at least by now, or at least courting. I didn't deserve to be his motivation, to be given such an honour. He was too good for me, and yet he thought otherwise.

My mind went to my mother and her fixation with class and status. She wasn't the only one but there was no way on earth she would have consented to me marrying a mill worker. I should have run away with Freddie and then Edward would never have been a temptation.

Freddie was too young, but he would have made a fine soldier. Strong, tenacious, brave, he had every quality required, and he didn't even need to try. Oh, the bitter irony. Freddie had far more class than all the Edwards of this world sewn together.

I touched his face then gently and blinked more than once to stem the flow of tears. I didn't want to alarm him, and I simply couldn't allow the floodgates to open.

I simply couldn't because I knew by then if I did, I'd never find the strength to slam them shut again.

Chapter 8

"I've told you enough times, Dorothy, you must run any extravagant household expenses by me. I'm not made of money as you seem to think I am. Things have changed since the glory days of your father."

"I hardly call new curtains for each room extravagant, Alfred," my mother snaps back, almost slamming her sherry schooner onto the side table.

Her hand goes to her pearl necklace, a sign she's agitated, making it appear as though she's clutching her chest in pain. Oh, father I wish you would learn to read the signs, I think.

"I would agree, but you've got expensive tastes, and you know it, and there's," he pauses to count on his fingers, "twelve, no thirteen rooms in this house for pity's sake!"

Tired of yet another heated discussion about the household finances I retreat to my room hearing my mother tell him the same thing she always tells him. She reminds him he's not the keeper of her livelihood, let alone her life. I worry the bitterness will choke her one day if my father doesn't see to it first.

Never was a bedroom such a haven. I'm so happy to leave the quarrelling behind and instead think about Janet and Larry's wedding tomorrow. I have important things to attend to for their big day. Betty has already carefully hung my lilac bridesmaid dress on the back of the bedroom door in preparation. As I run the wispy chiffon material through my fingers, I picture myself walking ahead of Janet down the aisle then waiting for her to join me to finally start living her dream. Her path of true love has been solid and straight and it has been a pleasure walking beside her to where she was always meant to be … with Larry as her husband.

"She's got good taste has Miss Janet, I can't lie," Betty told me when she saw the dress.

Janet loves the grandiose title of 'Miss Janet' and always looks over and smiles discretely at me when she hears it.

Betty has also been invited to the wedding, which has irritated my mother, and she's been planning what to wear for the special occasion for weeks. Janet and I snook off with her for an afternoon's shopping in Leeds and treat her to afternoon tea at *Harriet's* silver-service café. We finished the day with a glass of sherry.

Although she wouldn't hear of it at first, I'd given Betty some extra funds from my allowance, and she chose a dress of the palest green with a white satin trim to the neckline and cuffs. The pleasure was in the giving when I saw her face as she emerged from the changing room. I owe Betty far more than a few extra shillings for a dress.

"It's a shame your parents can't come, Miss Delfina, what with your mum being out of sorts, an' all."

Her eyes twinkling as she said it, we're both looking forward to letting our hair down. Janet's parents observed protocol by extending an invitation to my parents and my parents did their duty by respectfully declining due to a 'prior engagement'.

I was thankful when my mother eventually allowed me to see Janet again after our enforced separation. I found out from Betty it was Janet's mother who landed on the doorstep to set my mother straight about one or two facts. Her mother was charming but even so, my mother didn't entirely believe her. I couldn't help being touched she'd taken it upon herself to defend me when she didn't need to.

"I'm surprised my mother let her in the house, Betty."

"Ay, well, she wasn't going to air her washing on the doorstep, Miss Delfina now, was she?"

I know all too well Betty would have fallen over herself to listen at the keyhole. I asked her how the conversation proceeded, and she told me word for word, mimicking my mother's voice for added effect.

My mother heard the same explanation as Janet on the long walk home that night: That I needed some fresh air and was escorted outside by the gentleman in question, who had the misfortune to then become involved in a scuffle with another man through no fault of his own. That will have been the gist of it, but I didn't use those exact words with Janet, or she would have laughed me into next week, to coin a phrase of hers. This left only the minor stain on my character of going to a pub in the first place. This charge was one Janet's mother saw the funny side of as she'd been young herself once, she said. But she was wise enough not to say this to my mother. Oh, to have a good laugh about it, about anything at all with my mother. Janet is blessed with her family.

As for more recent troubles, only my mother and I know the full facts about this; Janet played no part in the sorry situation, so we're back on track as best friends. I haven't been able to bring myself to talk to her about Edward and I doubt I ever will. How to begin such a conversation.

I'd seen Edward a few times from afar over the last few months but only once came face to face with him and Susanna in the village. I was making my way back from Janet's house and as I turned the corner onto Main Street I met them slap, bang, head on. No place to hide, nowhere to run without creating an awkwardness which might raise alarm bells.

"Effie, how lovely to see you! My, you are in a hurry," Susanna said, her face as alarmed as mine but for very different, innocent reasons.

"Good afternoon, Miss Rogerson, Mr Cooper," I said inclining my head, "I apologise, my mother is expecting me for dinner is all."

How serene she looked smiling my way. I searched for polite conversation.

"Are you quite settled into the mill house?" I asked.

She nodded, saying, "Yes, Janet's parents are most accommodating. I almost feel part of the family."

I could smile broadly at the comment, albeit briefly.

"Yes, they have that effect on people."

We laughed together, my laugh tentative and hers genuine, crinkling the corners of her eyes.

I could see Edward watching us from the corner of my eye. I stole a quick glance. He had on a dark suit which made his hair look all the fairer and I looked away when his eyes met mine. I so wish I hadn't lost control to look his way. He hadn't forgotten about me; I could see it as plain as flour. I sometimes wish he would forget about me and sometimes I cannot bear that thought but surely it would be easier if we could forget about each other.

Instead, I find myself thinking of him at ad hoc times of day, or worse in the middle of a long night. Then I wake to the fact he's there, just a short distance away, when in truth he's gone forever. I've tried to think of him as the womaniser he is, but my emotions are complex, unable to be turned off. Like a leaking tap, they constantly drip, drip, drip away.

Susanna's faraway voice startled me.

"Well, we must get back ourselves and I wouldn't want to be the one to keep your mother waiting," she said, her voice teasing.

I didn't have time to think about my mother's reputation clearly preceding her because I was busy with thoughts of Susanna and not just her, thoughts of Susanna and Edward. They were dashing somewhere as a betrothed couple, perhaps sharing a meal together around the kitchen table in the sweet little schoolhouse.

Tomorrow they would wake to begin the fresh week ahead making wedding plans and other plans for a life … together.

The happy, carefree joke about my mother was from a woman who had the world in her palm. Yet, Susanna was unaware she was also the woman who had sole custody of my own world.

The only option I had left was to walk away with a cheery smile and allow her to cherish my world for me on my behalf.

Chapter 9

The old woman rests her head on the back of the chair. She looks comfortable but alert and as I study her face, I realise I'm becoming accustomed to the stain on her cheek. It no longer unsettles me.

I don't wish to know the time. The new year is due or perhaps already upon us, but all I know is I don't want this night to come to an end.

There are long pauses between her questions as though she's giving great thought to each of my answers before moving on. I feel significant, important even and I think she knows her opinion of me can go some way to either restoring or shattering the brittle self-belief I still have intact.

"You'd like to know what happened to my face," she says suddenly.

I'm relieved finally to have the chance to discover more, and although it wasn't said as a question, I nod my head at once unable to hide how much I want her to tell me. I would never have asked but I do so want to know.

Her eyes hold mine. I see many unknown thoughts passing through them like clouds scuttering the sky.

"I think your need is greater than mine at present. You've shared the significant events of your life and I understand why you've needed to, perhaps for many years. We mustn't stop the flow, break the spell. Not now.

How wise she is, how intuitive.

"Were you eventually able to carve a life for yourself without thoughts of Edward intruding? I hope so."

A sigh escapes me as I cast my mind back to that time once more. This is painful and complicated to unravel, even more so to try to explain to another person.

*

"Janet and Larry's wedding day was a day to remember for a number of reasons, some you would expect and others not so much," I tell her, "I had a lightness I hadn't had in such a long time. I was nineteen years old by then, but my mother was still treating me like an errant child. I know there was good reason, but I wasn't sure how much longer I could continue my penance.

It was a bright, sunny September day, so fitting I thought for a bright sunny couple. Their love was as fresh and clear as a sparkling stream, nothing to sully or cloud the water.

I arrived early at the mill house and Susanna greeted me as she headed out of the door.

"Good morning, Effie, you look very pretty," she said, "The house is bursting at the seams with people in there. I hope you've prepared yourself."

"That's exactly why we decided I should get ready at home," I said, smiling.

"I must dash, I have a train home to catch to visit my parents, so I hope you have a wonderful day. Don't get tipsy mind," she said, shaking her finger.

We giggled like two old friends. Yet, my hands were shaking and clammy, as I felt terrified of saying the wrong thing and tripping myself up.

I watched as she walked away, carpet bag swinging in hand, then braced myself for the hustle and bustle inside.

There were plenty of introductions and compliments from people who I had never met before to weave through before I could finally make my way up the stairs.

Janet was using her mother's room to get ready, and I patted my hair as I knocked on the door.

"If that's you again, mam, I'm nearly done," she called.

She had an irritable edge to her voice, and it made me smile thinking she will have been sick of her mother fussing and fawning over her all over morning.

"It's me, Janet," I said.

Janet came into view little by little as the door slowly opened. All sign of irritation had left her face by the time I had a full view of my best friend, and I couldn't help but literally gasp at the sight of her.

She made the most beautiful, radiant bride I'd ever set eyes on, eclipsing even the model brides in the magazines we'd bought in Harrogate and poured over endlessly, seeking inspiration.

I wasn't expecting us to have time alone, so it was an unexpected pleasure. Her mother made no bones about telling me Janet had ushered everyone downstairs as they were getting on her nerves.

"My, my you look a picture of perfection," I gushed in genuine admiration.

I stood back to take in the splendour of her borrowed dress. Silk and lace stopped just short of her slender ankles, her veil hanging in soft folds to her hemline.

"You scrub up alright yourself," she returned the compliment blushing awkwardly, so unused to being the centre of attention, "that colour's such a lovely contrast to your dark hair. You'll show me up, you will, Miss Delfina."

I shook my head at such a notion.

"Ready?" I asked then.

"Almost ready, just my lipstick. I wasn't going to risk getting it on this dress or my Auntie Audrey would have my guts for garters.

She finished her lipstick by pressing her lips together, then Janet looked at me standing behind her in the mirror.

"Now, don't let me catch you and Freddie playing footsie on the top table later," she teased.

"Footsie? We'll end up talking brewery business by the end of the day, no doubt," I said.

I would be secretly disappointed if that was the case.

She read my mind.

"I certainly hope not! I'll have no business talk at my wedding, thank you very much. Right, I'm ready as I'll ever be so let's face the bloody madhouse downstairs."

Smiling affectionately at my friend, we lifted our dresses at the knee then held hands to go down to join the mayhem. I couldn't have been more delighted for her. She'd waited patiently until Larry caught up with what everyone else had known from the very beginning: that they were a match made in heaven.

"As he makes them, he pairs them," was the phrase Betty used when I told her about their engagement, "I thought Larry was never going to cotton on. Mam said he needed his head felt if he didn't pop the question to Janet, she's a rare gem."

It was dreamlike listening to my friend saying her vows to Larry in the stillness of the village church; the atmosphere was thick with emotion as the marriage was a long time coming by usual standards. She had her back to me, but I could see Larry was moved by the sentiment behind his bride's words. Life would be different now, but I wasn't losing a sister, only gaining a friend.

The sudden sensation of being watched nudged me from my trance and I couldn't help but turn my head in Freddie's direction. His cheeky wink startled me, making me smile and look down at the fresh carnation posy clasped in my hands. All eyes were on the happy couple, so it was our own private moment. I glanced up at the best man again. He looked handsome, properly handsome in his new suit having grown into himself the last couple of years. A stirring of something pleasant took me unawares.

We'd had no end of conversations in his office at Braithwaite's and his name was regularly mentioned in despatches by my father during our short journeys to and from work in the car. He'd already made quite an impression with him and the staff at Braithwaite's. It was no surprise. Freddie was solid and straightforward, likeable.

"I think he's got his head screwed on right that lad, Effie," father confessed, "he's young but he's keen and capable. To be fair, I could say the same for you too, you've surprised me how you've taken to brewery business. James and I were talking about you yesterday—were your ears burning?"

"Goodness, high praise indeed, father," I said, laughing to cover my embarrassment.

I didn't know they were taking note. Such a glowing compliment from my father surprised me, especially as he lived and breathed Braithwaite's. I should have known the direct way to his heart would be working there. He patted my hand, and I watched him as he was driving, his chubby, ruddy face making him appear older than his fifty-something years. There was quite an age gap between him and my mother, I remembered. I thought then of her comment about people living fine without love. It made my stomach flip to think of such a waste. It was a waste of a life to me, but she would have thought that melodramatic nonsense.

One thing was certain, I'd never find out if either of them had loved and lost but I doubted it. I found it impossible to picture my mother as a young giddy bride with all her life ahead of her. I wondered if she'd ever even been girlish in her youth. How bitter she had grown in her ill-matched marriage.

And how sad it made me to think a person might go to their grave without experiencing real, genuine love.

Freddie and I danced the night away at the wedding and nobody batted an eye because it was expected of the best man and bridesmaid. We'd had some fizzy wine with the wedding breakfast which to my mind tasted far better than the expensive champagne we drank at home on Christmas morning. Like most of the guests, we were both tipsy by the end of the evening, full of laisse faire because real life was set aside for a while. Tomorrow seemed a long way away.

"Larry's looked like the cat who drank the cream all day," Freddie said.

His arms were around me for one of the slower dances. Janet had given me some dancing lessons, but I was far from a natural like she and Betty, so I was glad to slow down. The peaceful easy feeling was being in Freddie's arms, not just from the effects of alcohol.

Earlier the villagers were showering the wedding couple with rice outside the church and Edward was one of them. I thought of Susanna being away at her parents and him being alone. He had no need to come to church.

I gripped Freddie's arm tighter when I saw Edward watching me. I think perhaps I just needed his additional support at that moment. Freddie smiled down at me, and I couldn't help myself beaming back at him, carried along on the wave of the new bride and groom's happiness. I was soon self-consciousness under Edward's gaze which spoiled my mood and upset me that, even after so long he could manage to spoil what was set to be one of the best days of my life.

"Well, he has got the cream with Janet," I said with pride, "he knows which side his bread is buttered, he's not daft."

Freddie threw his head back laughing at my turn of phrase and I loved it. I even perfected the accent for added effect.

"Miss Thornton-Braithwaite, what would your mother say hearing you talk in such a way?"

"When the cats away…" I said, looking up at his face split by a playful grin.

His smile dropped suddenly then. He saw something in my expression as he stared down at me. If we were alone, he would have kissed me, I know it; he had that intensity in his eyes you have before closing them for a kiss. One thing was certain, I wasn't going to risk going outside with him again. Even with his curls flopping on his forehead and his shirt sleeves rolled up to expose those muscular forearms, even with his tie hanging loosely, his top button undone, I couldn't be tempted again.

Touching a tendril of my hair, he studied it curiously, telling me, "I think the next wedding we dance at will have to be our own."

My eyes floated around the dancefloor to be sure nobody was looking. I wasn't as taken aback with such candidness as I was used to Freddie wearing his heart on his sleeve when it came to us. It was as if he thought there was no reason to hide his feelings any longer after years of silence. His love was solid like him, something to cling to, something to depend on.

"Frederick Walker, is that a proposal?" I asked.

My voice was hoarse. So, this is it, I thought. This is the monumental moment of my life, where I'm asked to join heart and mind forever with another person, to become whole and as one. Was this how I imagined the moment? Perhaps not, but then it felt right, like my hand slipping into a snug, warm mitten, so it surely had to be right.

"I think my prospects are good enough now, if you'd like it to be a proposal," he said.

He stopped our dance, his eyes roaming my face, trying to gauge my reaction. I thought of his prospects, my mind then wandering to my parents tucked up in their separate beds in their separate rooms. He might pass muster, at least with my father, and sadly that was all that really counted at the end of the day.

"Well, kind sir, if you'll be good enough to escort me home, I will give you your answer."

A spark of delight appeared behind his dark eyes. They held mine as he raised my hand to kiss it gently, oblivious to onlookers. Within a few short moments, onlookers were of no concern to us any longer. We could hold our head high and look to the future. A sudden relief at finally being able to turn my back on my old life washed over me.

Janet and Larry had left the celebrations in a taxi, suitcases in boot, tin cans clattering, to head to the train station to set off on their honeymoon in Scarborough. They left showering everyone with smiles and kisses of gratitude. The last thing Janet did at the door was throw her wedding bouquet. I'd caught it with ease I remembered. Everything was suddenly making sense.

"I'll miss you, but you won't miss me," I told her laughing, "and if you do there's something not right."

"Oh, you'll be too busy over the next couple of weeks to think about me," she replied.

She drew me close and pressed her lips to my cheek, her carefully applied lipstick long gone.

It was a throwaway comment, the hidden meaning going over my head at the time, but later I realised she and Larry had obviously been party to Freddie's plans.

Freddie's urgency to leave the party was clear as we said our farewells. His arm strung over my shoulder he cut the pleasantries a little short for comfort, but nobody was in a fit state to notice or care.

"I'll be on parade in the morning first thing, don't you worry, Miss Delfina," Betty told me.

She looked as though tonight's 'one too many' might be a source of regret when she woke up in the morning. Her elegant feather slide had slipped to stick out just above her ear, giving her the look of a budgerigar, which had toppled off its perch. The likeness made me smile at her warmly, and I wished then she worked for me. I'm certain I'd be able to rustle up some breakfast to give her a later start, or even the day off. I freed myself from Freddie to clutch Betty to me, and she left her arms around my neck for the longest time. We said so much without the need for words.

When we separated, I slipped my hand into Freddie's like we did it all the time. What a difference a day can make.

I often think back to that night. I wonder if I had a premonition, perhaps some kind of sixth sense.

It just so happened that not so very long afterwards, my heartfelt wish for Betty's future came true.

Chapter 10

"How dare you, how dare you even ask the question of me? You snapped my heart over your knee like a twig," I say.

I almost hiss the words as I'm unable to shout. Edward's face is grey and drawn, his cheeks slightly more sunken than I remember.

"You're quite right, I'm ashamed of myself but I must speak with you and explain. Please Effie, our ending came about so suddenly and there's so much I would like to say, not just for my own benefit, for both of us."

For two pins I could lie down. I'm so hungover after Janet and Larry's wedding, I'm struggling to think of anything else.

"I'm heading to Janet's house for aspirin as the chemist is closed, I thought the walk might clear my head. Really, Edward you do pick your moments, I feel positively dreadful. This is the morning after the night before. Yesterday was quite a day."

He's staring at me. Does he think if he stares long enough, I will give in,

"I have aspirin at the schoolhouse," he says.

My face burning, I look down at my feet. I know Susanna is visiting her parents and we would be alone. This is too much.

"I don't think that would be a good idea," I say.

He locks his palm around his throat and sighs. How desperate and frantic he seems when I look up.

"Please, Effie, this may be our last chance."

The pounding in my chest and the wavelike movement in my stomach are clear indications he still has an effect on me. I should never have allowed him such power, I should have been strong, sent him packing when I first discovered him squatting without rights in my mind.

But I shall never find peace in my mind if I don't find out what he wants to tell me.

"I will speak to you, as you don't look yourself, but only briefly. I must get home."

"Thank you," is all he says.

We both look up and down the street to check for passers-by, but it stands deserted. Most are in bed nursing their sore heads after last night's shenanigans, exactly where I should have stayed.

I follow him to the rear of the schoolhouse, my eyes peeled for any onlookers. I'm on full alert until we're inside the walled yard and still I look over my shoulder as I follow him into the house.

We walk through the cosy kitchen I'd imagined the day I'd bumped into him and Susanna in the street. The room is different to what I expected but still cosy—a real family kitchen.

Edward heads down the hallway and into the front room. He puts a match to the fire in the hearth and I watch the flame kindle avoiding eye contact.

I sit rigidly in the chair as he sits opposite. We both keep on our coats as though we might need to flee the house at any moment. We may need to. We have yet to utter a single word since we left the street.

Time is of the essence as my mother will wonder where I am. She doesn't know about Freddie's proposal as he has yet to ask father.

I raise my eyes from the floor and look Edward straight in the eye. I really am in no fit state for beating about the bush.

"As I say, I'd be grateful if you could be brief. I don't have much time."

He cups his chin, then pauses to search for the words. I wonder if his pose is theatrical, if he's rehearsed it, prepared for this very moment. Theatrics or not, he must know we need to stop this. We simply cannot continue to float around the village, haunting each other.

"We're taking a risk in just being here Edward," I remark, untwirling the silk scarf from around my neck, the heat building in the room, "Susanna could find out I've been here. Such carelessness could lead to consequences. A tarnished reputation is one thing for you but…"

I stop speaking as he shakes his head madly as though ridding the awful thought from his mind, then tells me, "I understand, yet the risk is easy to take because the alternative is impossible to bear."

Impossible to bear? I bore the alternative, Edward. I continued to live my life, even when you were never far from my mind.

"Edward, it was a schoolgirl crush on a handsome teacher, a scenario played out that becomes dull in the cold light of day. You were old enough and wise enough to know this … and to not to act upon it."

His hand reaches out suddenly to cover my own. The warmth of his seeps into the coldness of mine and I sink into the sensation for just a second before somehow gathering my wits. I swiftly pull my hand from his grasp.

He is undeterred.

"Do you really believe this to be the truth of it, Effie? It was never my intention to seduce you. You talk of us taking risks but the hold we have over each other is profound. I wasn't leading you down the path to abandon you at the end, my feelings were just as powerful as your own."

He drops his head, his voice lower, less coherent, "You cast a spell, I tell you, and however much I want to, I'm unable to break free. Like a thirsty man craves water, a starving man, food, I crave the nearness of you."

I can sense the earnestness behind his words, they move me, but I'm at a loss. He could have had me, oh but he could, still he chose not to rock his boat. He can flower it up all he wishes, but that was what it all boiled down to. But I just can't bring myself to say the words aloud, to rub salt into the wounds of a battered, wounded man.

"A year has gone by now, time which will never return," I whisper to soften the impact, "a year when you should only have been thinking of your fiancée. I thought you were getting married, but I wonder if you have been putting it off. Susanna is a good, kind woman who deserves better. She deserves to have all of you, Edward, just as Freddie deserves to have all of me."

"You're preaching to the converted, Effie, don't you think I know all this?" he wails, his expression frantic, frustrated I think at not being able to make me understand, "don't you realise I want better for her, for me, for you, for all of us, but how can I make it stop? In the night, I wake and lay staring into the abyss of the ceiling, seeing only your beautiful face, staring back at me. Believe me when I tell you I've tried to make it stop. I've considered running away many times, with or without Susanna, but then there would be no sight, no hope of you. I'm stuck fast with no chance to run because I'm unable to break free from the tethers of my own mind. You have no idea of the torment I've lived through this last year."

His distraught words touch a place deep within, making me uncomfortable. I watch almost as an onlooker, as I reach out to touch his tortured face. I have an instinct, an uncontrollable instinct to try to soothe him in some small way. The responsibility is a burden that I'm the only person on earth who has the ability to soothe him.

I'm sickened by a sudden realisation: If I care about him so much, I must surely still love him.

Edward closes his eyes, nestling into the tender comfort of my hand on his cheek. It feels different to before, thinner and flattened somehow, as if I'm touching the face of a person who is fading away. I can't seem to drop my hand, to take this small comfort from him when he's clinging so tightly to my compassion.

"I love you, Effie," he says, his eyes tightly shut, his head moving as though trying to shut out the pain from even thinking the thought, saying the words aloud. Leaning forward his lips touch mine, but instead of responding as I would have done once, the feel of his lips brings me to my senses. I step away quickly as though they have burned me and hear a small gasp as his eyes search my face for clues as to why I could reject him.

He is too late. This moment has come too late for us, because now I have someone else who loves me, trusts me.

I shudder when I think of the loving expression on Freddie's face when he proposed. I should not be here; I should not have let Edward persuade me.

I race out the back door and down the back lane to run like the wind. I must take myself as far away from temptation as possible.

Because now there is Freddie.

Chapter 11

The old woman now knows I was tempted to cross the line. I am compelled to confess as any omission tonight would be the same as a lie.

I clear my throat, unable to continue the excruciating silence any longer.

"I can imagine how disappointed you are in my weakness," I say, "but you must believe me when I tell you I've since discovered the worst disappointment of all is the disappointment in oneself."

She's considering her response carefully and I'm unable to meet her eyes.

"It is patently obvious you regret your decision," she says eventually, "I doubt any discussion on the matter could make you feel worse than you do already…or indeed any better. I will only say this; you seemed impetuous, easily led by others, both are traits of youth."

My mother's face springs again to the forefront of my mind as it so often does. I see her admonishing me as a young girl in the sitting room of Carleton Hall, her face a mask of rage. I was horrified but I now find it odd these temperate words should affect me far more.

We have broken down a barrier and drawn a line under what I needed to tell her. She waits until I'm ready to continue and I think how lucky I am to be sitting here tonight, having such a conversation.

I will be forever grateful for this opportunity to offload the distress which has been part of me for so long. This is laid bare, and now I am finally ready to face it and relive the next part of my story.

*

The voices are muffled through the wall but certainly getting louder.

I've never heard James raise his voice to my father, or anyone else in all this time. He's softly spoken generally, the voice of reason. When I glance at Freddie, he remains frozen in his seat, but I step out of his room to walk down the corridor and listen through the jamb of the door. I can't help it; I must know what's being said.

"Why the hell didn't you tell me, Forrester?" my father booms, "I thought the opportunity was in the bag, ours for the taking. You made it sound like we'd no great competition, at least none to lose any sleep over."

The volume of my father's voice shocks me, so I take a step backwards. I consider running back to the safety of Freddie's office but now I'm the one who's frozen. I need to know more. It's clear something terrible is afoot for Braithwaite's.

"No, it wasn't in the bag at all, that's just what you wanted to hear. You came to that conclusion without a shred of evidence to back it up. I've told you many times we've been skating on thin ice, but you refused to believe me."

His voice had dropped slightly but James's exasperation was still clear from his tone. I suspect he's done his best to warn my father, but he's been in denial. We were the top-seller in our region for a hundred years, so why would a blip mean a permanent decline, is precisely what he would have been thinking.

"Like I told you, we should have moved to mechanisation earlier. The competition saw the opportunity and seized it."

"You and your bloody efficiency. Our beer's still the best in Yorkshire," my father says, interrupting James. Braithwaite's has been here a whole century, they know us."

"Yes, it is, and they do. But it isn't enough, Alfred," James says, his frustration pushing his voice up a couple of notes.

"*Bass* are offering the free houses kegs at far less than us and they're offering to cover the costs of buying out some of our managed sites. How can we compete with that? Don't take it personally. To the publicans you're just another brewery bigwig in your castle. Don't get me wrong, there's still a fair bit of loyalty to Braithwaite's, but this is amongst the older publicans who your father-in-law signed up. Business is business, I don't need to tell you of all people this, surely."

I hear a noise like my father has slumped in his chair and then the ensuing silence is unsettling. I wipe my top lip with my forefinger. Normally, my father always has something to say for himself.

Freddie told me on the quiet it looked like sales had been dropping for a while and it was true; we hadn't kept pace with changes in machinery and transport. Even the *Crown and Cushion* right on our doorstep had *Bass* as a guest beer and Freddie said his pals preferred the competition. He only stayed with Braithwaite's purely out of loyalty. He and his friends were the future, not the old-timers who indulged in a couple of pints on a Friday and Saturday evening, then never set foot in the door for the rest of the week.

I hear an enormous breath escape James.

"Look, Alfred, I'll see about some advertising, but we must think about bringing in new equipment—keg filling, bottling and motors," he says, "my only concern is all this might be too little too late. We might just be throwing good money after bad."

"You should have had your wits about you, Forrester, that's what I pay you for, to stay one step ahead of the competition. Your wages might be throwing good money after bad."

My father's tone has a nasty, threatening edge and I'm shocked by the accusatory remark. This is below the belt and uncalled for. Nobody is more loyal and hardworking than James and my father's insult upsets me.

"Perhaps it's not the forward-thinking competition which will finish you, Mr Thornton, perhaps it will be your wife living beyond your means," James says.

James controls his tone, yet it does nothing to soften the barb.

I stifle a gasp, then fly down the corridor, straight past Freddie's office and back to my own so I can sit down immediately and pretend I haven't heard. I imagine James will shortly be leaving the room, voluntarily or otherwise.

All the time I'm running, I can still hear my father yelling, "Get your bloody things together and be on your way, you useless little weasel. What concern are my wife's spending habits to you? You're finished here and I'll see to it you'll not claw your way up another bloody ladder because you'll not even get the chance to sit at the bottom of one again."

I'm back at my desk quaking uncontrollably when the next thing I hear is James Forrester's footsteps thumping down the corridor and his voice commanding me to ring for an ambulance.

Chapter 12

Your wedding is all anybody talks about," Janet said, "Oh, how they've never seen a dress like it, or a more beautiful bride, or the village hall in such a state of grandeur. Grandeur's not a word I would ever have thought I would have used once to describe that tatty old hall."

"I imagine the revamp my father funded, along with the free food and drink for the village guests all day might have had something to do with it too, Janet," I laugh.

My father wanted to have the wedding breakfast at the hall, but mother asked who we would have invited other than an aunt and uncle I'd never met who lived in Doncaster, and James Forrester's family. The rest of the guests would be from Freddie's side and sparse. I think she just couldn't bear the thought of villagers traipsing about the grounds and poking their noses in every room.

So, my mother took the decision out of my hands. My aunt and uncle never made the short journey in the end.

My father consented to the union instantly, my mother pretending to deliberate, yet all the while knowing it wasn't her decision. She still wanted to flex her muscles, but Freddie's manner convinced her she wasn't taking on a nobody as a son-in-law. My mother's standards were discerning but even she could never think Freddie a nobody.

"He's a good-natured fellow, I'll give him that much," she remarked in the run up to the big day. Freddie laughed when I told him he was honoured because I couldn't recall her proffering a compliment about any other person before.

"He's fond of you too, mother," I told her.

She couldn't hide a small smile. I understood why Freddie would like her. She was different in his company; they had an easy-going way with each other, a natural way. I envied this sometimes because my life would have been much easier if I could have been on friendly terms with my mother. I think she would have fared better with a son.

"Well, he'll be master of this house one day, so it's just as well we can rub along well together."

Freddie, master? What a notion. I was set to inherit Braithwaite's and Freddie would never lord it over me. He's of a more enlightened generation to my father but, in any case, we had a very different kind of relationship. Ours was a little more on an equal footing.

Janet was right, the wedding was magical. It was only a shame the last memory of the day prevented me from basking in the glow of it for very long.

Before the ceremony, I'd taken my father's arm for him to lead me the few steps down the aisle to begin my new life as Freddie's wife. As I peered at him through my veil, he turned my way, staring at me as though seeing me for the first time. He smiled almost ruefully as I waited for him to speak.

"A day like today makes you reflect, Effie. You've found a good man in Freddie, he'll look after you, be there for you. I should have been around more at home I know that now, but I'm not sure if your mother would have thanked me for getting under her feet. The brewery is a poor substitute for a family, but I don't think I'll need to remind Freddie of it."

What a time for regrets.

"Don't be too hard on yourself, you were following in my grandfather's shadow and no doubt wanted to go the extra mile to impress him."

I fought the urge to tell him the truth. The truth was he really shouldn't be hard on himself as the hall was never a welcoming place to return to. But it was neither the time nor the place for such a conversation.

"I'm not one for sentiment as you know," he said, "but I couldn't be prouder of you and not just for making your mark with the business. I can't let the moment pass either without saying there could never be a bonnier bride. You look beautiful."

My throat caught as he looked away, eyes glistening with affection and more. I moved my veil aside to kiss him gently on his cheek.

He blushed then, saying, "Come on, lass, let's be rid of you finally."

We laughed together then, a good start to our walk down the aisle.

Then I saw Freddie, and he saw me, and the rest of the afternoon is a blur of wonderment. A good start to our new life together as man and wife.

It was the end of the evening by the time I found myself alone in the powder room, combing some semblance of order back into my curls and reapplying lipstick. It was time to grab Freddie and say our farewells; I was ready for home, *our* new home.

I caught my reflection in the full-length mirror and studied my dress of the purest white lace with a dusky pink velvet belt. My mother had seen it on the cover of her magazine, and had it sent up from London to Madame Giraud's, the wedding outfitter in Leeds. Janet moaned when she saw it the first time, telling me she wished she could have borrowed my dress rather than her Auntie Audrey's. The dress moved with me, and dusky pink hand embroidered roses skirted the hemline. My hair hung in curls to my shoulders, my veil fitting like a cap then cascading over one shoulder. Satin heels with a buttoned strap completed the look, which my mother described as understated yet classy. I was grateful to her for buying my wedding dress, she was keen not to skimp.

"Well, I only have one daughter and I want her to look the part on her wedding day," she said dismissively but then her expression was soft when I came out of the changing room in the full ensemble.

"From the day she's born, every mother lives for the day her daughter ties the knot. It's your day as much as theirs, she said running a finger over the velvet of the belt. This dress could have been made for you."

The run up to the wedding had been a happy time, but my wedding night couldn't come quick enough. It had been difficult to wait, with a few near misses over the year or so of our engagement. Freddie was all man, the epitome of masculinity.

I set off down the foyer towards the church hall with a sense of anticipation, keen to find my new husband and end the waiting game. I smiled to myself at the sound of the laughter and chattering of the guests still in full throng.

After only a few steps I stopped in my tracks. Somebody was loitering, I could see them out of the corner of my eye. They were clearly skulking, and I knew immediately, even before I saw their face exactly who they were.

My mother had invited Susanna and Edward to the wedding as she had no alternative. If she had crossed them off the list, people would wonder why, including Susanna. I imagined her addressing the invitation to Mr & Mrs E Cooper, and the memories it would have stirred for her.

Yet, here he was again, set to sour my day, but this time it wasn't any old day.

"Effie, please," he whispered to me in the foyer, "I know I've no right to ask and today of all days, but would you speak to me a moment?"

He must have seen a flash of something in my expression.

"I certainly don't wish to take you away from your guests for long," he added quickly.

I wanted to flee from him again, unable to bear the thought of my mother coming across us alone together. But more because talking to Edward was utterly pointless. What could he have to say to me and on my wedding day? No good could come from entering into a conversation with this man.

Susanna had gone home earlier in the day. She was more than halfway through her pregnancy and worn out. I had expected her husband to join her. Instead, he'd been propping up the bar all evening with Freddie's brother, Jack. I didn't even know they knew each other, or perhaps it was just a ruse to hang back. Shame on him if that was the case. Everyone was merry by then except Freddie. He was keen as I was to head back to the cottage we'd decided to rent in the village until we found somewhere permanent. We decided to defer our honeymoon to the south coast for a week or two so we could enjoy our wedding day to the very end.

We should have headed off earlier like Janet and Larry then Edward wouldn't be standing here waiting for my answer.

We stood face to face, my back to the room bustling with celebration. The outside door of the foyer was open, letting in a welcome breeze. I didn't want to look at him, so instead I looked down studying the scattering of delicate roses as my dress fluttered like butterfly wings in the breeze.

"You should have accompanied your wife home, Edward," I said dully.

"Why did you not tell me Freddie had asked you to marry him?" he asked.

So, this is why I'm here, I thought. I'm here to be interrogated on my wedding day.

"Edward, you would do well not go down this line of questioning. You do not have a leg to stand on."

He grabbed my arms.

"For the love of God, Effie, I can think of nothing or nobody else. I never thought you would marry Freddie."

My teeth clenched so hard my jaw hurt. I wrenched my arms from his grasp and stepped away, an anger flying up my chest from a place where it had been festering too long. How could he have such a conversation with me today? I struggled to keep an even tone, to hold on tightly to my composure.

"After you confessed you loved me, you should have told Susanna you didn't want to marry her but no, you were still hedging your bets, waiting to see if I would change my mind. Freddie *is* the man for me. You have some nerve to question me this way. If you really meant for us to be together, you should have been on your own instead of wanting the penny and the bun."

He starts to speak but stops when he sees me backing away.

"Regardless, I can release you from your ordeal, Mr Cooper, I am now a married woman and no longer available to you. And may I remind you that you were never available to me. I'd be grateful if you would let me go now to return to my husband and our wedding guests."

He stood firm, no sign of inebriation whatsoever.

"Tell me you don't think of me every waking hour as I do you, and I'll leave you alone for good."

"I don't think of you every waking hour," I told him flatly, my eyes looking over his shoulder, checking the function room for signs of life through the glass doors.

"I don't believe you, Effie. I'm sorry but I know you do."

I wanted to yell at him though it was out of the question.

"Are we going to run away into the night together, abandon your loyal wife and my adoring husband, not to mention your unborn child? I'm older and somewhat wiser now, Edward. We would never have worked."

Though I was unable to raise my voice, the words were delivered with such passion he could be in no doubt about my position.

His hands reached out then dropped instantly to his sides again, thinking better of it. He was unsure what to do, how to proceed and it made him appear lost and floundering. He had always been in the driving seat with us.

The doors opened, and the noise of the room grew loud. I swiftly moved away from Edward and was caught in a conversation with a tipsy Larry telling me it was the best wedding he'd ever been to in his life.

Up until two minutes ago, I would have said exactly the same. I hugged Larry to me and saw Edward watching us. Just go Edward please, I thought, and I meant it.

I left Larry and saw Freddie watching me too. He smiled then put on his suit jacket to head over to me.

As he walked across the room, our eyes locked and I pictured us both outside the back door at Carleton Hall after Janet and Larry's wedding day.

"Come on then, are you going to put me out of my misery?" Freddie asked me under the stars the night he proposed.

There he stood, the man who adored me. Freddie had been waiting expectantly for years to get my attention, then he had worked tirelessly to prove his worth to me and my family.

I made my decision.

"I would love to be Mrs Delfina Thornton-Braithwaite-Walker," I told him, tongue firmly in my cheek.

"Now, hold your horses," he laughed, "no wife of mine can walk about with a name like that, I think I might just have changed my mind."

Our eyes clashed and held fast, my expression turning serious.

"I would love to be your wife, Freddie," I told him.

I could feel his love for me, as our faces edged nearer for our first kiss. It was a gentle kiss which shifted quickly to ignite a sensation inside me, one I'd had before, only this time it pained me less. It left me wanting. I could sense his own want of me as his arms went around me to draw me closer. He was strong yet tender in my arms, baring his vulnerability. If we didn't glean some self-control, it would take us to another place. But that private world would have to keep for a while longer, I thought then.

I wish my head had been full of questions, those of our future and of my love for the man who I was set to spend the rest of my days with. I couldn't possibly live lovelessly like my mother. It would be like being starved of air, unable to survive.

Such a marriage was simply unthinkable.

Chapter 13

A question floats around us and I wait for her to speak it, stalling the moment.

"It will be no surprise what I'm about to ask you, I'm sure: Did you love Freddie?"

There it is. The question I've had so much time to mull and which I regretted not seeking the answer to all those years ago. Instead, I wanted rid of the whispers at the back of my mind and so I chose not to ask myself the question for long enough.

My throat is dry. I take a drink as I've already talked far longer than ever before in my life. My answer is readily available, it sits inside me, locked away long ago, never for one moment imagining it would be spoken aloud.

The woman's face is kindly, I can see no sign of judgement. To listen without this is difficult, impossible for most, and I value it. I had no idea it would be like this when I entered the cottage only a few short hours ago, mind and body aching and at the end of my tether. I wonder now if she has known love, so she understands, or if she has no experience of such things.

"No, I find it difficult to say, but I'm afraid I came to realise I didn't love Freddie, not then," I tell her frankly, matter-of-factly, though I am feeling neither.

Exposing what I'd hidden for so long is like the intense pain of ripping a gauze from a wound.

"But that changed after we married; I came to love him as he loved me," I tell her, "And I've no doubt I'll love him to the end, and I hope beyond."

She searches my face then nods, satisfied I'm speaking from the heart. I'm glad I've convinced her as somehow, I want her to think well of me, but certainly not at the expense of the truth. This would be a waste of a heaven-sent opportunity.

I relax a little and stroke my stomach gently with my palm, my mind swimming with thoughts and recollections.

*

"Freddie and I were content for a time in our little cottage. I took well to keeping house, finally tending somewhere I could call our own. Freddie's mother, Madge called every Saturday morning for tea, not too early mindst she told me, as she had chores to get through. She kept a nice home though she had been poor her whole life. Freddie and I treat her discreetly to little pieces for the house as she wouldn't hear of taking any money from us. I looked forward to Saturday mornings and talcs of the young Freddie and his brother.

"You never get two the same, lass," she said one morning, her huge bosom resting contentedly on her folded forearms as she sat at the kitchen table, "I can't see Jack ever settling like our Freddie, not since he came back from fighting. It's as though he's decided to live the life his lost pals will never have on their behalf. It's no secret his head is turned too easily by a bonny face as well. Pity the girl who thinks it will be different with her—she might be right for a Saturday but then who knows by Sunday. There's always a new one, a next one. He's too much of a looker and he knows it. But age is a great leveller, I tell him, don't grow old and fat because it's lonely."

I grew fond of Madge, and I looked forward to our cosy kitchen chats, finding her easy to rub along with the same as Betty. She got on Freddie's nerves a bit and she knew it, but then this is a mother's lot, you'll see soon enough she told me.

My father arranged driving lessons for Freddie and even bought us a little car, turning up with the keys and a case of beer one Sunday grinning from ear to ear. He increased Freddie's wages and my wages to make up for ending my allowance. He said he didn't want Freddie to think he couldn't look after me. I enjoyed my new life, coming home from a working day to the simple pleasure of homemaking. I tried out the fine recipes Betty passed on to me, I swept, dusted, polished— all new tasks and all satisfying. Freddie assumed I'd want to leave Braithwaite's, but I told him I was more than happy to stay on until we had a family. I'd grown to love my job and Freddie liked me around so we could lunch together in the canteen or if the weather was on our side, nipping off in the Morris for a picnic.

Janet already had a daughter, Rose by then. The prettiest little baby she was, the image of Larry, and well-loved and looked after by her doting parents even though I knew money was tight the same as it was for Madge.

"Won't it be smashing when we're both pushing our prams out together?" Janet said, "It would be like a dream come true if they grew up good friends like us, Effie."

We were having tea in her tiny front room swimming with baby paraphernalia, the kitchen almost filled by the new pram we'd given Rose as a gift. I thought I'd done the wrong thing to begin with.

"No, I can't accept it, Effie, it's too much. I'd never be able to return the favour."

She ran her hand over the navy-blue hood and silver metalwork in awe, shaking her head my way.

I was wrong-footed. Was it a little brash offering such an extravagant gift? I didn't intend it.

"You've already repaid me in friendship, Janet, and it was you who kept me from going off my rocker throughout the long years of solitary confinement. Please accept it, you'd make my day. Oh, I feel awful now."

"Ah, well, if you put it like that, how can I possibly refuse?" she laughed, self-consciously, throwing her head back so her strawberry blonde hair hung in a braid to her waist. She refused to have it cut as Larry said it was her best feature and he'd feel sick if she chopped it off to be fashionable. She told him off for being over dramatic, but he's right, it would be a shame if she followed the trend of having shoulder-length hair.

She placed Rose to her breast, already quite the expert, and I looked on with affection at them both. It was my turn to be awestruck.

I so wanted our baby to arrive before there was too much of an age gap at least. The niggle appeared again as I watched on. Six months had gone by with no sign of a pregnancy, and it wasn't for the want of trying.

Our wedding night had been well anticipated by both of us, and it lived up to our expectations, boding well for things to come. Janet had trimmed up our little cottage with extra candles and flowers and she had thoughtfully lit the fire in our bedroom.

Freddie carried me over the threshold and straight up the stairs to our bed, kicking the front door closed behind him and not even breaking his stride.

Lips clashing, we fell on top of the covers, hands exploring each other with a fire long-burning deep and fierce. I wanted him, I wanted him to be mine. He unbuttoned my dress, his hands trembling with the thought of our long-awaited pleasure. My arousal continued to mount as his fingers curled around my bare breast. I felt my nipples hardening under his touch, then I reached to feel his hardness under the firm pressure of my palm.

"My sweet girl, how long I have waited for this," he whispered, "I shall never be able to tear myself away from you again."

His fingers climbed higher and higher up my thigh to find their way inside me. A moan escaped me, and I thrusted my hips to heighten the sensation. Revealing him in desperation, I grasped his pleasure, and he showed me how to move my hand in such a way we both sunk into a mutual hunger, a desire for more.

His response was to lift my legs high, and I gasped at the first thrust. He waited a second and watched me to see if I wanted him to go on. It was my first time of loving, and so natural to have Freddie guide me and have complete trust in him. I left him in no doubt then that I wanted more, oh how I wanted him. I heard him moan in response to the movement of his hips with mine, locked in the gratification our bodies were offering each other. I passed to another world, dizzy with hedonism and something more—love. The crazy, crazed power of a devouring love. It had finally arrived to flood my heart just at the perfect time.

We cried out together, reaching the summit of our pleasure, and he delved deeper inside me before collapsing over my chest, his lips kissing my hair.

"In all the years I laid awake with you in my head, I could never have imagined how you could make me feel as your husband," Freddie told me, "It was worth the long, long wait."

This man loves me beyond my wildest dreams, I thought then.

"I love you, Freddie," I said quietly, unabashed.

He lifted his head to look at me and I touched the roughness of his cheek, thinking how ruggedly handsome he was.

"I could tell you I love you too, but that would never be enough, you know that."

How I did know that.

But even with such a perfect start to our marriage each month that passed brought an increasing sense of disappointment for both of us that a baby hadn't arrived to complete our little family.

"I know what you're thinking, I can read your mind, but six months is no time at all, you know," Janet said, "Winnie Franks took three years to have a baby if you remember."

Her face dropped and her cheeks coloured.

"Oh, me and my big cake hole. Sorry, Effie, here's me making you feel worse when I was only trying to make you feel better."

I patted her knee to settle her nerves, keen to pacify her with a smile.

"No, I think you're right. It takes time for plenty of couples, why should it be any different for us?"

Six months however turned quickly to twelve, and the niggle became one I was unable to shift. I continued working, glad of the distraction because the niggle was steadily progressing from a freckle to a wart. I wondered how long I could leave it before I had a proper discussion with Freddie. We were both putting it off, I knew we were, because we'd spoken of starting a family straight away before we married. We were all too aware of a problem and I for one was keen to look at how to fix it. If we at least laid the foundation for a path to follow, it would surely be more bearable was my thinking. Tiptoeing around the matter was tortuous.

Edward had a fine son by then who they named Daniel Edward and I'd seen Susanna in the village not long after he was born.

I allowed myself to look at the tiny new life, his mother lulling him to sleep in his pram with the sound of her soothing voice. The expression on her face was lovely, a proud new mother, ignoring everything around her until her son was content once more. A fine, strong name for a fine strong boy, with a coating of downy fair hair already growing as a gift from his father.

"He's beautiful," I told his mother.

I meant it whole-heartedly and not as a glib comment people make when we're shown a baby for the first time.

"Susanna was born to be a mother, you know, like some people just are," was a crushing observation of Betty's, and Betty was clearly right. She was a natural, her boy returning once more to a peaceful sleep, silky eyelashes spanning the pinkish cushions of his cheeks.

I only thought of Edward if my memory was triggered by then. A passage of a book might do it, a word, rainy weather perhaps, but it was fleeting.

However, it wasn't long before Edward was pushed even further down my list. Freddie and I found ourselves with more unexpected and pressing matters to address.

After the dreadful row with James in his office, an ambulance had rushed my father to hospital, but there was nothing to be done in the end. He died even before he arrived at the hospital the doctors said from a massive stroke. I knew he was dying when he passed me on the stretcher and I stumbled along behind, in a blind panic, pushing away offers of coats. Freddie pleaded to go with me in the ambulance, but I had a strange feeling I'd never had before. All I wanted was my daddy, not my father. I'd taken his protective presence for granted and then it was too late. This was smothering any other thought in my head.

The last person I saw as the ambulance man slammed the doors shut was James. He had the haunted, incredulous look of a kind, gentle man who had been thrown into the middle of a living nightmare.

I knew time was running out and there were urgent things I needed to say to my father whether he could hear them or not.

"I should have mentioned it before now, but you know we love you, don't you?" I said, tears dripping from my chin to land on his exposed chest. I somehow couldn't bring myself to just say, "I love you," even then, even at such a time. It was awkward to say it, and I wanted to spare him the awkwardness of hearing it. He was not a demonstrative man. This should not have been a consideration at such a time, but death can push your mind to strange places. How I know this now.

The rear of the ambulance was oddly calm as I held onto my father's hand, willing him to stay with me. I stroked his hair, then lay my cheek on the cold cotton of his sheet, so our faces were very close. I thought about the regret he told me of on my wedding day at not doing things differently at home. The sadness overwhelmed me that it had occurred to him too late, and my mother would not meet him halfway to make amends.

He rolled his eyes my way for a brief second then closed them again, but I was certain I felt the gentle squeeze of his hand at the time.

I still like to think so.

I will always refuse to believe it was only my imagination."

Chapter 14

I swallow noisily and hold my breath. I must subdue the tears, the tears which are constantly waiting in the wings to make a dramatic appearance. They've been patient for many a year.

The woman's mouth is set, her eyes circles of concern. She understands because she will have endured the loss of both her parents. The thought of such a lonely, empathetic lady living such a reclusive existence upsets me. Though perhaps she isn't lonely at all and prefers to live her life in solitude. Solitude is far different to loneliness because you choose the former, whereas the latter chooses you in circumstance.

No words from her are necessary. How can a person speak to you so eloquently without words I wonder?

I close my eyes and rub the side of my face. I'm struggling to compose myself, but I must if I'm to continue onwards with my tale.

*

"Freddie became the man I always knew he was after my father died. He stepped up to the plate, taking care of all of us, at work and at home and my mother gladly leant on him more than I could have imagined.

Not surprisingly, she became a different person but not gradually, it was almost instantaneous. Grief can make you behave out of character but if she didn't love her husband, it was a peculiar kind of grief, thinking more about herself rather than mourning his loss. Freddie missed him professionally, but I mourned him. I was the only one who mourned the person he was.

James however was guilt-ridden. He was the one who had given him the cold, hard facts and the poor man thought he had personally delivered the fatal blow.

"I don't blame you, James," I told him, at the hospital, so eager to offer him reassurance, "the conversation you had was long overdue, and the reality of the situation would have come to light one way or another. The Board has always had complete faith in you, as do we. I hope you'll stay and help us try to rebuild Braithwaite's."

He touched my hand, a hesitant feather-like touch, but it was as though he'd drawn me to him in a warm embrace. The stark greyness of his pallor lightened just a little like a cloud had lifted slightly. Would he ever forgive himself? My words would only go so far in easing his guilt.

Freddie and I were the only ones who knew about the heated exchange, but we agreed James certainly wasn't to blame and no-one else needed to hear of it. No, what killed my father was his lifestyle. A lifestyle of over-working, over-eating, over-drinking, in fact general overindulgence, and not a few choice words.

And a few choice words which just so happened to be true, at that.

Poor Freddie has been handed an impossible task. Braithwaite's empire is crumbling, and he's been thrown to the helm without preparation or warning, to try to lead us through the storm. His lack of experience is obvious, and he sees this as losing face, pride making him think this is somehow a slur on his standing as a man. Now I know a man's pride is forever burning like a fever which can burn to the point where they lose all reason.

Our lives have become unrecognisable, and we too have become unrecognisable, from the newly weds who enjoyed a humble life in their little cottage like the rest of the villagers. Those times, that couple, they seem a distant memory. I miss them.

"What time can I expect you home?" I ask yet again.

I hate the words immediately, the simple question layered with hidden meaning, and I'm bothered by it most as I sound like my mother.

I don't know what to do. I can feel it, the slow resentment festering in him. But surely, I can't change the state of our marriage on my own.

"The same as last night and the night afore," he snaps, "you'll be tucked up in your bed sound asleep, so I always wonder why you seem to care so much."

He's fastening his laces, head bent, a disguise for his expression. I breathe out long and steady through my mouth, eager to control my response. I really don't want to fall out. I mentally begin counting to ten but I'm unable to finish as I've no time to lose. His mind is already out of the door ahead of him.

"Only I was thinking you could come back a little earlier that's all, or even give yourself a night off. We need to talk, Freddie, you've been trying to push everything further and further to the back of your mind, but we must talk."

He stands up but won't look at me.

"Talking, talking, talking, it's all you want to do. It won't change anything, and you won't change my mind either."

I'm not startled by his tetchy tone as this has become his default mode of communication of late. A tetchy tone or a simmering silence is all he offers me, and I don't know which is harder to deal with.

He's clumsily stuffing money in his wallet from the desk drawer of his study, still determinedly avoiding eye contact. He wants to run away from me, this house, Braithwaite's … from everything. I think how proud he was to have this room when we moved in after my father died, telling me it couldn't be true. That it was a room full of class, and history and it belonged to him. He's barely in the house nowadays, never mind his study. How on earth did we get to this point I wonder yet again.

A flicker of strength appears from nowhere, and I touch his arm. I must make him look at me.

"Freddie, you know you're drinking too much for your health, and our wealth for that matter. At this rate you'll have us on the streets. I don't have to hammer it home again surely that life is far from what it was in the beginning. We must tackle the issues head on while we still have the option."

I'm stating the obvious again I know, my frustration coming to the fore before I have a chance to quash it. I don't want to add to his worries, but is it even right to always quash it?

He shrugs my hand away and I catch the look in his eye, the one invariably just below the surface. I plant my feet and raise my spine to square up to my husband, waiting to lock horns and for battle to commence. I can't allow this cycle to continue but it seems I'm alone in trying to break it.

Spinning on his heel he strides towards the study door. He just can't face going over the same argument again and I understand this well. When he glances over his shoulder, he looks at me as though he hates me. But I know this is not the truth of it.

Oh, Freddie, I know the truth is that you hate yourself.

"Don't wait up," he calls from the hallway.

He almost slams the back door on his way to his second home, *The Raven*. The village's only pub 4has become his refuge, somewhere to burrow himself away from the harsh realities of life. I'd like to find a refuge of my own.

He's gone and now I'm left helpless. Whilst ever he is here, I still think we have some hope. I want the gentle easiness of daily life back before the pressure began to alter him. The changes were subtle to begin with, so they barely registered at first. He started to call in for a 'swift half' on his way home, which was fine but then this evolved into being late for dinner. When my mother had words, he came home for dinner then went out until closing time. We speak at work but only about business and there's no avoiding the state we are in. The outlook for Braithwaite's is bleak.

I miss our shared banter, our moments of flirtation where he would gently push me up against the wall when nobody was around at work and fondle my breasts which were bursting to be rid of the buttons of my prim blouse so he could get his hands on them. Where he would tell me what he planned to do to me in bed or even beforehand that evening, so I ached to be alone with him until we finally left the office together.

Mostly though, I miss our togetherness.

My evening's confinement now stretches uninvitingly ahead. The house isn't empty, but it has the cold, dismal atmosphere of emptiness. My mother settled herself down earlier for the night in her self-appointed wing of the house.

"You're the head of the household now," she said when I moved back home after my father died, "I've arranged for the attic to be made into a living area. The space is huge and unused up there and I don't want to step on your toes down here."

I was uncomfortable being the one in charge of the household, the decision-maker. I respect her as my mother, and I would have been glad of her guidance, especially in the beginning.

More than ever, I wanted the homeliness of our cottage back. The cottage was my refuge though I didn't need it then.

"You won't be stepping on anybody's toes," I insisted, "we're out at work all day and even if we weren't, it's completely unnecessary. It would be lovely to live together and work as a team. You know how highly Freddie regards you."

"A husband and wife need privacy and to be honest, so do I. My home has always been Carleton Hall so I cannot contemplate leaving but I still need some space of my own. A house could never run smoothly with two mistresses, it would never work."

More illusions of grandeur from my mother. We don't live in a castle or a stately home and the wonder that she is, Betty is all we have. We don't have a team of staff from housemaids to butlers to footmen. But I couldn't persuade her, and she ensured she had her space and plenty of it.

Any company would be consolation right at this moment, however. The clock on the mantle strikes eight as I head up the two flights of stairs sitting between us. I knock and wait, admiring the patina of the oldest door of the house, always respectful of the boundaries she set. I wait for her to grant me permission to enter her world.

"He's gone out again then I take it."

The flat statement was on the tip of her tongue, and she's been waiting to release it, barely waiting for me to get my foot over the threshold. I wonder if I detect a hint of disdain or even a slight whiff of self-satisfaction all is not well downstairs. The fire's blazing in the hearth and she's wearing her cream velvet robe, sitting on the second settee she took from the front room to limit expense. She's replaced the silver cover over the remnants of the meal she ate earlier, the one Betty prepared and presented. She would never take the plate downstairs herself and she would never hear of me taking it downstairs on her behalf such is her belief we all have a correct and proper role to play within the household. Two pin curls poke out from the top of her turban headscarf. Betty will have set her hair before dinner.

My mother isn't quite the same force to be reckoned with now my father's no longer with us. It's become apparent so much of her confidence relates to status and wealth. I never feel like I'm the Lady of the Manor and I never will, she's welcome to the title. Occasionally she'll wander downstairs to eat with us, usually on a Sunday but she's very concerned about being in our way and soon retreats up here.

"Yes, he's called for a pint with Larry."

Of course, this is the truth yet only the bare bones of it. I want to tell her everything. I want to explain why Freddie's avoiding the situation we find ourselves in. Over twenty endless months have passed since we married and now, and I don't recognise my own life because every aspect of it has changed.

Instead, I ask if she has everything she needs before I retire for the evening.

"You'd do well to get the situation in hand if you know what's good for your marriage. You can give a man too long a rope."

The thought of taking marital advice from my mother makes a shiver run down my back. Though her eyes never look up from her magazine, I know she holds me accountable. I'm the one to blame.

The room has lost fresh air, so it's stifling.

"Yes, I'm content thank you, so I bid you good night," she says.

I have been politely dismissed. The coldness of her tone can be withering at times.

"It's not what people say sometimes, it's the way they say it that cuts you," Madge told me before she left.

She moved to live on the east coast with her sister, Freddie's aunt, because of her bad chest she said. In truth, along with Jack we were working all week and her days were long. I called in when I could, but she didn't like coming to see us at the big house as she called it. My mother wasn't entirely welcoming, but to be fair, she did try to be for Freddie's sake. It didn't translate well, Madge is more sensitive than she appears, so she could see right through the pretence.

The days of the cosy chats by the kitchen fire with my mother-in-law are long gone. If I thought she could make Freddie see sense, I'd write to her, but he'd just see this as a betrayal. I can't risk adding more fuel to the fire.

"Goodnight, mother," I say.

I'm glad to step out of the room and I stand for a moment in the draughty hallway of the attic and think how she's always been a closed book and not just with me. She's been acting out the roles of wife, mother, head of the household within the confines of her own definition. Yet, she's been distant even from the people who should be pivotal to her life.

I want a child. I close my eyes to the overpowering longing taking my breath, so I lean against the wall. I need a child. I want to do motherhood differently, to make them feel the love I should have felt, as all children have a right to feel. I want to be a mother like Janet's, Betty's, Freddie's—they are all fine role models.

Freddie must talk to me soon or I will crumble.

Does my mother wonder why we haven't yet presented her with a grandchild? Is she indifferent to the trials we're facing or is the question steadily choking her?

I wrap my cardigan tighter around me as a shield from the cold of the attic and the realisation I'll never find out the answer to those questions, like so many others.

Chapter 15

Betty only calls twice a week to clean and batch-cook nowadays. She's one of the sacrifices we've been forced to make and the one I miss the most, though not for her housekeeping skills.

"If there was any way that we could keep you on full time, Betty, you know I would. You've always been in my life like family, a second mother even."

I don't want her to have any doubt about the place she holds in my heart. I'd hate to regret the missed opportunity of never speaking the words aloud. I said too little too late to my father and I will not make the same mistake again.

"Ay, I know, and I feel the same," she says.

She blushes then heaves a sigh. As she holds onto her chin deep in thought, her coarse reddened hands are a contrast to the paler skin of her lovable face. Those hands have cared for me my whole life and I love them for it. I can almost see the cogs turning and wonder what's on her mind.

"Now look, Miss Delfina, I've lined up a house to clean each day and I'll probably have more once word gets around that I'm available. Me and mam don't need much to get by so don't you fret about me, you've had enough slapped on your plate, enough to outface the best of us."

She's studying me closely, her eyes scrolling up and then down again, making no bones about the fact she's giving me the once over. Her eyes mist before she drops her head.

"It's you I'm worried about," she whispers, "I'd be obliged if you'd let me speak plainly while we've got a moment alone. I'm worried sick about you, I really am. You're too thin, stick thin, and … and I've heard rumours about you and Mr Freddie."

She reaches to touch my arm, to soften the frankness of her words.

"I'd be a liar too if I didn't say I've first-hand knowledge about some of their tittle-tattle. I've got eyes in my head, I know a lot of what goes on in these four walls," she pauses, "about his behaviour towards you."

She puts her tea towel down to give me her full attention. I'm awkward under such scrutiny, and I'm not sure what she's heard. I thought we were hiding our situation well, but you can't hide from Betty, she's far too incisive.

"You shouldn't listen to gossip, Betty, it can be misleading," I laugh nervously to cover my discomfort.

I really don't want to talk about it, not even to Betty for once. Staring at her from my favourite spot to chat at the kitchen table, I hope she'll help me out and change the subject.

"Well, I might as well tell you what Larry's been saying because it might help you to know what's going on. Mr Freddie's been getting some ribbing about 'firing blanks' as they call it. You know what men are like, big on humour and short on tact, as my mam says. Anyway, what with one thing and another, I think life's all getting a bit much for him."

Firing blanks, what an expression. I know immediately who the instigator of the unfounded accusation is likely to be. Thomas Baker is still a dark cloud on the horizon. I still can't draw Freddie into a discussion about our difficulties, let alone undergo any tests. I went to a consultant in Leeds on the quiet and he told me the problem doesn't appear to lie with me. I just can't find the words to tell him. His virility will be in question, and this is a nasty little pill for any man to swallow. So, I can't think about anything else, and I've run out of ideas. I used to have the odd glimpse of the old Freddie, but he now seems to have long gone.

Betty made scones earlier as she knows warm scones are my favourite and wanted to encourage me to eat. I've been nudging one around my plate, so I don't offend her kindness, but the sight suddenly makes me queasy. I sit back in my chair unable to play the game any longer and push my plate away.

The other thing she's referring to is Braithwaite's.

"Braithwaite's is going down," is the whisper around the village and beyond. The reality is I don't know if we'll be able to see out the end of the financial year. I haven't told my mother for many reasons, only speaking about the problem with Janet. She keeps me up to speed with the whispers about the brewery but keeps her powder dry regarding Freddie. He's Larry's best friend so she wouldn't want to betray him, and I understand.

We're clinging onto the grim hope the advertising campaign James Forrester has invested in will halt the slide whilst we try to secure some investment for new machinery. But everyone knows we're not living the dream they thought we lived any longer. The cutbacks we're making aren't even scratching the surface of the problems we're facing. Seventy-eight men are looking to us for a way out. That burden along with the state of my marriage and the longing for a child rotate in turn to the front of my mind. It's like I'm on a terrible fairground ride and screaming to get off, but nobody can hear me.

Then before we even dared to hope for a brighter future, James delivered his bombshell: he's leaving us to go to the competition. He said he's taken us as far as he can, and the opportunity is there to be had now but it may not be in the future. To be fair to him, he has a family to support and after weighing up the options he's decided to jump ship. I'm not sure though how we can keep the brewery afloat without James on side.

There's no point in us feeling angry and betrayed because deep down we can't really blame him.

As for Freddie, he may as well have jumped alongside James. He's given up on Braithwaite's and without him he'll be thrashing about in the unknown. Still, stubbornness is making him push me away when we should be clinging to each other at such a time. Only we know how bad life is, and we could be supporting each other until we get to the other side. What lies on the other side, I have no idea, but get there we must.

"You can tell me anything, Miss Delfina, don't forget," Betty says, "loneliness is a slow drip of a torture, and it can make us do things we wouldn't normally do."

My eyes dart her way then drop. What does she mean, does she know more than I think? She remains quiet, but I can't muster the correct response.

Finally, she pats my hand before grabbing her coat from the back of the door.

As the familiar sound of Betty's footsteps on the gravel drive ebbs away to quietness, the loneliness she was so keen to mention takes hold.

I watch the sunlight stream through the window and think it may as well have iron bars upon it.

The bedroom is in silent darkness when sometime after eleven Freddie returns. Force of habit makes me close my eyes as I hear him coming upstairs and I feign sleep. I do this every night but tonight is different. I don't understand why tonight would be different to the hundreds of others before when I catch a whiff of Freddie's breath brushing my face. When he shakes my shoulder from behind, my eyes open wide to the intrusion, the sudden trampling down of my private barrier which kept me safe for so long. Why tonight, why not last night, the one before?

"You wanted to talk," he says, too close to my ear for comfort, "so talk. Let me have it then, go on. Talk, the right honourable Mrs Braithwaite-Walker. I'm very interested to hear what you have to say for yourself."

I sit up in bed, drawing the covers up under my chin. I'm shivering from cold but more from fear. He's so intimidating in drink, a loose cannon, unpredictable and out of control though he's never laid a finger on me.

"Freddie, please, now isn't the time. Just go to sleep and we'll talk properly in the morning."

Stumbling around the bed, I see he's in no mood for reason.

"No, it's now or never. I've got plenty to say before you do, so you'd do well to let me get it off my chest."

I keep quiet and my silence is more of trigger than words. Flopping himself down heavily on the eiderdown, he then drops forward to place his head in his hands. He reminds me of a sulky little boy.

I brace myself for some home truths which are heading my way. Although I'm fully versed with them, it will still be uncomfortable to hear.

"You blame me for all of it, I know you do. The state the brewery's in, the upset between us, all this is bad enough, but I know you blame me most of all for not giving you a child. You're desperate for me to be prodded and poked by a doctor just to prove to you I'm the one at fault. I can't do it, Effie, don't make me do it."

He rubs his hands forwards and backwards over his scalp, trying to rid himself of the distress.

"I can't face the humiliation, I tell you, and worse still, I can't face the consequences if I can't give you a child. But don't you see, if a miracle were to happen, how on earth can we afford to raise a child with financial ruin only a hair's breadth away?"

Though he's drunk, he still raises a valid point. It might be wise not to engage with the conversation, only listen—a drunk is not the best audience.

But his pain is mine and I can't help wanting to try to take it away.

"I don't blame you for any of it, there's no fault to be had, not for either of us. I just want to find out why we can't have a baby. I'm desperate to know if we have a chance in the future even if we aren't blessed with one right now. Is that so wrong of me? As for the brewery, we both know it was on its knees before you took charge."

The words fire straight from my heart before I have time to think about them.

He turns the top half of his body around to look at me. In the gloom I can see raw pain behind the wetness of his eyes. I want desperately to take it away. I know I still have the power to do this for him. He needs me, my husband needs me, my throat catches at the realisation.

His eyes follow me as I climb out of bed, unsure what I will do next. I see his thighs, powerful and strong, the sight of them arousing me now. I cup his face between my palms and stare into the deep pools of love-light I swam in so long ago. The light is shining my way and still only shining for me, nobody else.

"Freddie, my Freddie, I can't bear to see you in such a pit of despair. I would dearly love us to have a child it's true, but I love you more. You must believe me if we're to have any hope of being content. Somehow, we need to find peace of mind and we can only do this together."

I kiss him full and hard on the mouth, feeling closer to him than I ever have. He's shown himself vulnerable to me. A sob escapes him as he pulls away and draws me to him. I wonder again why tonight is different, why tonight is the night he's chosen to drop his defences. I've waited so long for reconciliation, recognition of a problem even.

With one faltering forefinger I gently slip each strap of my nightgown from my shoulders, so it drops to the floor. It reveals every part of me to him as an offering. A veritable feast after months of famine.

Dropping his head forward between my breasts, he mutters, "I don't deserve you, Effie, you're too good for someone like me. I don't know how this has come about. Sometimes I think I'm living a dream which is fast turning into a nightmare. I want it to stop and to go back to how it was in our little cottage. We were so content then."

I stroke his hair as his tongue now reaches for my nipple, the bud swelling into the warmth of his mouth. I have the awakening I had the first time he kissed me but nowadays I no longer need to hold back. Pushing him backwards, I quickly pull down his zipper then take him fully and firmly in my palm. I hear him moan as he closes his eyes thrusting himself, so the rhythm steadily builds. I desire him just as fervently as he does me and I climb onto the bed to straddle him, legs bent either side of his hips. I expose his broad chest after undoing the buttons of his shirt and gently stroke the dark hairs, enjoying the softness beneath my fingers and the masculinity he exudes. He lifts my bare buttocks to slide me into the perfect position to take him inside me. I arch my back and moan my pleasure as I rise and fall above him. He closes his eyes and reaches to fondle my breasts as we both build into a frenzy of pent-up passion. We've been starved too long. It has been too long since we took comfort in each other. I think of our wedding night when I was waiting to give myself to him completely. He's shown me how to love him as a woman and I do this now. Our passion continues burning brightly with each thrust until he shudders his release into me. I fall forward and bury my head in his shoulder.

"I love you. I love you, my beautiful girl," he whispers to me in the darkness, "please don't ever leave me. For richer, for poorer, for better, for worse, I'm unable to live a life without you by my side now. You have every reason to go but stick with me, please see it through."

I'm thrown at such a proclamation, praying he's speaking hypothetically, and I haven't given him any reason to think such a thought.

"I love you too, Freddie," I whisper, and I feel the words which are so easy to say now because they are the truth. I sense the enormity of them.

Truly, I am trying with all my might to block out the image lurking in my mind of the man who waits outside our house each night. The one who stands staring at me from behind the yew tree as I draw the curtains. I'm trying to block out the aura of his obsession with me.

I'm not sure how much longer I can wait to venture into the grounds to plead with him for all our sakes to forget me, to move on with his life.

He must listen because his behaviour is scaring me. But Freddie finding him out there watching me is scaring me more.

Chapter 16

My patience is waning because I have so many questions, but I follow her lead. I know I must as she is in charge.

The fire is still roaring up the back of the black leaded grate, but the lantern at the window has long since burnt out. The room should be eyrie, ghostly even yet it isn't. The atmosphere cocoons me. I am safe and sound.

"Do you think you encouraged his obsession, even stoked it in some way?" she croaks, her throat drying further in the heat of the room.

"I ask myself this often. I'm not sure how I could have encouraged him. We never interacted, never spoke in any way. I chatted to Susanna occasionally if it was unavoidable but never to him directly. Perhaps though my silence was permission."

I watch her intently as she gathers her thoughts.

"It may have been in everyone's best interest to send him away."

She is insightful. I waited too long and now I must live with the consequences.

*

"The night Freddie and I rekindled our passion I slipped into a peaceful sleep thankful we had finally turned a corner.

Then the morning after when I awoke to an empty bed, I knew immediately I was back in the wilderness. He had dressed and was downstairs ready to go to work when I joined him. My suspicions were only confirmed by Freddie being unable to meet my eyes and our stilted conversation; we were back to square one. It was as though he'd slept on his words and decided it best to pretend that they were never spoken, or perhaps drink had distorted his memory. Either way he'd swiped his promises cleanly off the table. I'm sure he remembered at least some of what he'd said by his evasive manner, as though I'd forced him to show me too much of himself. The light I had glimpsed at the end of the tunnel went out which was far worse than never seeing it at all.

It took me two more days to broach the subject. I studied Freddie's profile as he drove the car confidently to work, his eyes fixed firmly on the road ahead. His strong silhouette was like a bust—set and free of expression.

"Freddie, I don't want to keep raking over old coals, but I wonder why we haven't spoken of the conversation we had the other evening."

How ridiculous a wetness should appear on my top lip when I was only talking to my husband. It was because I knew it was my last opportunity to speak or forever hold my peace. I was sick of hearing my own voice.

"I wondered how long it would take," he said, never taking his eyes off the road, "Effie, don't you think we have enough bother without adding to the list."

His irritability was clear. So, in a few words I discovered his real thoughts on the subject. It stung that Freddie could refer to any baby of ours as a bother when having a baby was all we could talk about in the early days. Couples on the poverty line had babies, loved their babies, and thought becoming a parent was the best thing they had ever done. Janet often didn't have two pennies to rub together from Tuesday to Friday evening when Larry tipped up as she called it, but they were happy as a summer's day.

I should have vocalised my hurt, but I was too deflated to summon the courage. Instead, I said something more benign, less pivotal.

"I wish things were different. Not just for me, for both of us."

He briefly glanced my way, his taut expression relaxing slightly. I think by my remark he thought we were on the same page. I was only too relieved to have diverted a confrontation to realise.

I wanted to lay my head back on the seat and close my eyes. I was suddenly tired, feeling far older than my twenty-three years. I'd been browbeaten into submission and resignation by my husband. A husband who was living in denial or even defeat.

That autumn was as cold as winter itself. Christmas was a long time coming. The hall was a façade, beautifully decked for the festivities when nobody in the house was remotely festive. I decided to throw myself into preparations and remembered I'd uncovered some treasures in the attic when my mother was converting her living area.

However, trimming the trees and collecting foliage from the garden to make garlands was an all too brief distraction for me.

Janet called on Christmas Eve as she knew I would be alone on what should have been one of the most sociable nights of the year. A night to share with the special people in our lives.

We targeted the advertising campaign to happen during the normally lucrative Christmas period. It was perfectly timed, and though we could ill-afford it, we hoped the campaign held the key to all our futures. After a sullen drive home, Freddie insisted he was just having a couple of pints at *The Raven* but promised he'd be back by half-past eight at the latest. He didn't want to miss the festivities he said, and I couldn't have been happier to hear it. Larry was at home babysitting Rose, forgoing his night out with his friends. I imagined him eagerly awaiting Janet's return.

On the journey home, I'd watched the thickening of the snow enhance the already picturesque village and wished I was looking forward to the break like the brewery staff. They had been full of banter and anticipation, not getting much work done, just the same as every other year. As always, we finished the day with beers and mince pies in the boardroom and the mood was lively. I certainly wasn't in any hurry to head home.

Colin, our head brewer said he was hosting a party. The staff had been talking of us being in the local newspapers and on billboards for weeks and found the prospect of fame a source of hilarity.

"Fancy old Braithwaite's being splashed all over the papers," was the consensus. The advertisement consisted of a man looking lovingly at his beer glass in a country inn, the strapline reading, "Bully for Braithwaite's."

No-nonsense and straight to the point, very Yorkshire, but it still cost us two hundred and fifty pounds for three advertisements in the Yorkshire Post, billboards across the region and on the side of the omnibuses in Leeds, Bradford and Sheffield. All we could do was pray it was an investment worth making.

"You're both welcome to join us," Colin said, "It will be a bit of a squeeze in my cottage, but the more the merrier, I say."

His voice held a slight note of apprehension that his offer might actually be taken up.

"Thanks, Colin," Freddie said from his office, "but we already have plans for the evening. Take a few cases of beer home with you to jolly the party along though."

We didn't have plans. Freddie and I should have been hosting a party at the hall, never mind Colin. The hall was big enough, and it would have been a nice gesture for the staff who were uncertain of their future. Perhaps it was for the best as the fuddle would be sorely lacking in the jovial atmosphere which Colin would no doubt provide.

In the early evening, Janet and I had a sherry by the fire and a slab of Christmas cake Betty made months ago with slices of Wensleydale cheese atop. The fire was crackling cosily in the hearth, lighting the room along with the candlelight. The tree was nine-feet tall and accompanied the twelve-feet tall tree twinkling in the hallway. The local farm donated them to us each year as a long-held tradition. We were never more grateful for them than this year with money being tight. Betty, as custodian of Christmas decorations until recently had taken great care of them, treating them as her own.

The hand painted drummer boy stared down at me from the mantle. He was almost as good as new though he'd taken a battering when Freddie knocked him off the shelf in a drunken row. He'd forgotten how he'd carefully repainted him when we found him amongst the box of treasures, telling me he couldn't wait to show our little boy or girl how he worked one day. He wound the key in his back, and we watched on with childish joy at how he marched and tapped his drum in time to the tinny music.

After the little drummer boy was smashed, Betty collected the pieces and glued them back together to return him to his position without fuss. It was as though nothing had ever happened. He looked the same as before but no longer worked, he could have been symbolic of our marriage.

My mother had dinner with us and then headed upstairs to spend the evening alone. She didn't bother decorating her rooms, not really caring much for Christmas. She never really cared for Janet either, still holding a grudge in thinking her commonness led me astray years ago. Janet didn't care much for my mother either so at least there was no love lost.

Whilst reliving the day I hadn't noticed Janet had been quiet for some time. We seemed to each be in a world of our own and I rushed then to break the silence.

"I was wondering if I should go to Colin's party for a while. I think it only right I make an appearance when he offered. I'd like to show willing and thank everyone for their support, particularly over the last few months."

I'd noticed earlier that Janet had a pensive look about her, as though she had something she

154

wanted to get off her chest. I just hoped she didn't want to ask about Freddie. I couldn't face it. She was wearing her red woollen skirt belted at the waist, with a cream cotton blouse and a hand-knitted cardigan in a lighter shade of cream. The ensemble looked new and very appropriate for the time of year.

"You look very festive tonight," I said.

Sighing, she put her plate on the side table and sat back in her seat. She looked at me briefly then immediately looked away, so I became the pensive one. What could be on her mind?

"Is everything alright, Janet?" I asked.

I thought she needed a prelude to the conversation because she clearly didn't know where to begin.

"Well yes and no," she replied, "I…I've been trying to think of a way to tell you, but I can't help feeling bad. I've never kept a secret from you before."

Looking down at her hands she was obviously struggling to say the words aloud.

She was pregnant.

If I hadn't been so preoccupied, I'd have noticed the certain glow she had when she was expecting Rose had returned.

Something more powerful than envy appeared. Surely it couldn't be jealousy—I had never been jealous before. If it was, I never expected Janet to be the one to introduce me to it. I was shocked and ashamed, so it took me a moment to dig deep to find a smile for her. It wasn't Janet's fault I couldn't find that certain glow I yearned for so much it was like an ache. It wasn't her fault the glow remained out of reach and seemed destined to stay there.

"I'll spare you feeling awkward about the announcement, even though you should only be delighted; I'm delighted too for you both, for all of you."

I hope my smile didn't betray me and delight really was all she saw. It was muddled with so many other thoughts and feelings I was having trouble fathoming. I had a slight sense of injustice of the fact she already had a devoted husband, that she already had a beautiful daughter. I tried to ignore the dreadful fear I was destined never to announce to the world that I was to be a mother. I would have sold my soul to do it once, twice would have seemed greedy.

I pinned my smile in place as I rose to stoke the fire. The contrived distraction would soon be over and then I would need to force myself to sit down and ask all the usual questions you ask a mother to be.

Of course, I did ask the questions, and she dutifully gave me the answers, but it was obvious she didn't really want to because she felt sorry for me. Last time she was pregnant we'd both jumped up and down in her kitchen holding hands when she'd told me the news. She told me even before her family because we were that close. Our bond was so special.

Now I was uncomfortable and trapped like a feral dog, backed in a corner not knowing whether to growl or whimper to make my escape. I wanted her to leave, so I didn't have to process all my complex emotions in front of her when all I should really be experiencing was joy. Pure and utter joy.

"Well, I must be on my way, Effie," she said only moments later, "I've so much to do before the morning because we need to wait until Rose is in bed nowadays."

"I can imagine," I said, nodding. I wanted the night to end, for us both to put each other out of our shared misery.

But of course, I couldn't imagine as I didn't have any experience of making sure your children were in bed to prepare for the arrival of Father Christmas. I had no experience of them waking at the crack of dawn to jump on your bed with excitement and wonder.

"Merry Christmas, Janet," I said.

Though my mind was elsewhere, I was trying my best to disguise it from her.

"Merry Christmas to you too," she said.

She opened her mouth to say something more but thought better of it.

What was she going to say, I wondered, did she hope next year I would be in her shoes or was she going to offer her commiserations? Either way,

I was glad she'd been thoughtful enough to let me off the hook.

After a brief, uncomfortable embrace, Janet almost tripped over her own feet, scurrying down the hallway towards the front door. Grabbing her coat and scarf from the hall stand, she bundled herself into them while I stood there watching, trying to think of something to say.

"See you soon," she shouted too loudly over her shoulder and set off down the steps at speed. She must have checked herself because then she started to walk more slowly down the snowy driveway, and I was relieved as she didn't only have herself to think of. How terrible it would be if she fell because she was running away from me, running away from her best friend.

And she didn't turn to wave at the gate as usual.

I closed the door and leant against it. I wasn't prepared for the turn of events that evening, but by then I wanted to do it all again immediately so I could do it right. Janet shouldn't be worrying about my reaction at such a happy time, and I already wanted us back on track. I would've liked to have run down the street after my best friend and ask forgiveness, but I somehow couldn't move. Time was important now or I could risk making a bad situation worse.

Janet thought she understood. If anyone could empathise it would be her, but someone could never understand such a longing when they had never experienced it. The only thing I did know for certain was that I would never have wanted my best friend to live with such a pain and neither did she.

I headed back into the front room, not entirely sure what to do with the rest of the evening. How empty the room was, yet picture perfect, just waiting for Christmas joy to flood into its four walls. I fought back tears then at the thought of going up to bed alone on such a night.

Nine o'clock, a half hour after the time Freddie promised to be home came and went unnoticed as I pondered on earlier events. At quarter past, I went to the window to draw the curtains on another Christmas Eve. Curtains in hand, I peered into the glistening nightscape.

Of course, he was there. I knew without question he would be. I knew he'd be watching the house from the cover of the yew tree, and he would have been there for some time even in the snow. He'd surely gone mad.

Janet would never have seen him as he was clever in the spot which he chose so he could quickly hide out of sight especially if Freddie returned home unexpectedly. I wondered if he'd already had to hide on such an occasion.

As I drew the curtains, I raised my eyes and blew out a weary sigh. I stared at the floral pattern of the fabric without seeing it, thinking all the while of what I must do. I positioned the fireguard, then went into the hallway to don by warmest coat, scarf, and fur-lined boots, focusing only on the task in hand so I didn't change my mind. It had gone on long enough, I needed to address the situation that very night. The door was slightly swollen and stuck when I tried to open it, but only briefly. I then flung it wide with conviction to see the figure waiting out there. Come what may, this must be done, I thought. What lay ahead for me after the address, only tomorrow would tell.

With hindsight I now believe the slight delay in leaving was sent by fate or some other higher power for a reason.

I would have done well to stop and listen to what it was trying to tell me."

Chapter 17

She shuffles to a wooden chest and pulls out two woollen blankets. The room is warm but not warm enough to stop me shaking from reliving the news of Janet's pregnancy.

As she hands me a blanket, I smile weakly with gratitude, placing it around my legs. She does the same and we settle down into the comfort they bring.

"You feel ashamed by your reaction to Janet's wonderful news," she says.

I don't respond because this was a statement of fact. Instead, I play with the woollen tassels of the blanket, the threads sliding through each finger in turn are soothing me.

"Your friend knew how you felt. Knowing and understanding still does not make us react in a perfect way. She was as out of her depth as you were. If the situation was reversed, you would have felt the same as Janet and vice versa. Longing is far more than an ache it is a pain and a constant one at that. Emotions are complex, at any one time we are rarely feeling only one emotion. If we are, it is fleeting as the brain is constantly moving."

She speaks articulately, and I understand the message she's trying to relay.

"Your words bring me as much comfort as this blanket," I say.

"I'm glad to hear it, but this does not make them any less true."

Her mind has moved on already I can tell as she stares at me, a demonstration of the brain in constant movement as she has only just explained to me.

"What happened when you left the hall that Christmas Eve?" she asks.

I gently gnaw my bottom lip. Every stage of our journey is becoming harder to tell.

"That Christmas Eve, I strode down the wide steps of the hall with purpose. The freezing air blasted and burnt my cheeks, but I barely noticed in my mission to put a stop the madness.

Edward stepped forward from the tree as I approached and then we both stopped in our tracks to stand face to face. I took in the sight of him. He was so near, free from the glass shield of the window, and yet he looked so different.

I cocked my head once, instructing him to follow, and he walked silently and obediently behind me towards the grounds at the rear of the hall. I couldn't risk being caught with him by a partygoer on their way home and especially not by my husband returning from the pub. Edward was close behind, clearly eager to speak with me. So, his perseverance had worked in his favour in the end … or so he will have thought.

I doubted by then that Freddie would be home before midnight as on Christmas Eve there was always a lock-in at the pub after closing time. The police would be turning a blind eye or even joining the gathering given half a chance. If he came home earlier, I'd simply tell Freddie I called in to show solidarity at Colin's party. He would have completely forgotten about my absence by morning. The same way he completely forgot about our reunion only a few short weeks before.

I turned to face Edward once more, the man looked frozen to the bone.

"Well then, I would be grateful if you could explain to me why you've been hounding me every evening? Have you lost your mind, Edward, I'm not sure what you think can come of it," I said.

Those were the first words spoken to each other since the night of my wedding. I hadn't seen him up close since then and I scoured his expression for clues. He was even thinner, I noticed, some might even say gaunt. His eyes hollowed and sunken watched me closely.

Taking a step backwards I did my best to put distance between us.

"How to answer such a direct question when any answer I offered would be inadequate. Before I attempt, it would be better to know if you're expecting your husband to return anytime soon. I'd prefer not to rush my explanation."

I sighed knowing he knew the movements of my husband as well as I.

"Is Susanna not expecting you home anytime soon? Is she not waiting for you to return to her and your son this Christmas Eve?" I asked, "I cannot imagine where she thinks you go every evening."

His eyes widened, taken aback by my scalding words. He should have been ashamed, leaving his family every night only to watch my every move. He should have been tucking his son up in bed, reading him a story. I would have given my eye teeth to have the opportunity.

His woollen coat, the deepest shade of navy like a midnight sky, had seen better days, much like the man wearing it. I thought he'd return to Susanna and his humble yet respected life of a village schoolteacher, content to be a husband and father. He had a reprieve as my mother only wanted to brush our liaison under the carpet. Rumours never surfaced, so he could just continue with his reputation intact. I took the opportunity to do the right thing and he should have left me in peace to live my new life with Freddie.

Except he could not see me happy with another man, which was the long and the short of it.

"Well, as you're keen to bring up the subject, Susanna thinks I go to the pub each evening like most men around here. This isn't something a wife questions, as you are all too aware."

It would surprise him to know I had questioned it. The pub had become Freddie's 'other

164

woman' and she was driving a wedge between us. Ironically, my father never went to the pub, calling it a busman's holiday when it was full of employees ready to give him a piece of their mind when they were full of ale. They had little to complain about then, but as he told me once, being the one who sets the rules makes you unpopular for that very reason.

Oh, Freddie I thought, your refuge should be your wife and your home not the pub.

Tears burned my eyes and Edward saw them, walking nearer to console me. I was too quick and sprung away from him.

Unsure what to do next, he decided to stand still and wait.

"Go home, Edward," I said quietly.

"Please don't send me away, Effie, not tonight. I love you the same as I ever did. Nothing has changed for me."

I groaned loudly and dropped my head back, startling him.

"This is my point, you say nothing has changed for you, yet don't you see, everything has changed? We are married, tied to another. We made vows and I intend to honour them even if you don't."

I was tired. Tired of trying to convince a man who refused to be convinced.

"Do you love me?" he asked.

"Edward, have you not listened to a word that I have said? What is love without loyalty, devotion, commitment to stand by each other when times are hard? I love Freddie."

He needed to hear me say the last part of my speech, I realised, he needed to know where my loyalty lay. I loved Freddie as a woman loves a man, a wife loves a husband, not as a child loves a fairytale which is all we ever were. I stared at his wounded eyes in the darkness until I could bear it no longer. Starting to walk up the pathway I turned to see if he would follow me. My heart hammered when he didn't make a move for the longest time, and all I could hear was my own breathing. I willed him to go home and leave me alone.

Finally, he made a move, and I stepped to one side to allow him to pass. I fell back and leant against the wall of the hall watching until he disappeared from sight. When he was finally gone into the night, I hung my head with utter relief that the encounter was over.

Standing at the rear of the house I spotted the Christmas lights in the hallway and tried my best to ignite even a flicker of a festive spirit. I lifted my head higher to see our bedroom then higher still.

In the attic window I caught sight of the outline of my mother's face, staring down at me from her room.

Although I couldn't see her expression in the darkness, I could picture it well enough in my mind.

Chapter 18

"A strained Christmas came and went, and I was only glad to see the back of it.

Then, at the beginning of January my mother became unwell with a chill which progressed steadily to pneumonia despite frequent visits from the doctor and a stay at the cottage hospital. She was away for some time but when she returned, she was so worryingly frail I stayed home more to take care of her.

Freddie was just as preoccupied and distant but for once I paid little heed to either mood because I was at risk of losing everything. The 'everything' included my mother and although we had our differences, this was still an unbearable thought.

The advertising campaign turned out to be a fruitless waste of time which was hard enough, but it also took our last pot of money. The situation was grim, and the bank finally called in our loan. We couldn't pay and administration loomed.

All we had left was Carleton Hall. It was an asset but in my mother's name, and therefore not a company asset, so we didn't have the worry of losing our home at least.

Even if we had considered a sale to save the brewery, it wouldn't cover the debts and there was a further consideration … it would have finished my mother.

Edward was still skulking the grounds even after everything I'd said and was clearly deranged. However, his obsessive behaviour simply wasn't as troubling any longer. Edward was a grown man, and I had a man of my own whom I loved despite everything to worry about.

Instead, there was another person continually on my mind. I thought about them more than Freddie even each day. She crept into my distressed mind one long night and stayed after a conversation out of the blue with Betty:

Susanna.

Betty was the only person who noticed how the strain of it all was taking its toll. Freddie chose to ignore it, unable to look at it or look at me.

"Sit down before you fall down," Betty said, pulling out my seat at the kitchen table.

I couldn't argue. It was the first sunny morning after weeks of bad weather in late March, but it had barely registered. My dress was too warm for the unexpected change in temperature, and it was hanging from me because I was "all skin and bone," as she'd told me more than once. Nourishment was the last thing I was concerned about, some found comfort in food in distressing times whereas it only sat in my craw.

"You need to get off to your next house, Betty, you do too much for us as it is. Don't make me feel guilty for holding you up."

"I keep telling you the same thing over and over, I'm out of my mind fretting about you, Miss Delfina, it's awful to see how bad things have got for you and Mr Freddie. I've told Mrs Fairstone in the village I'll do my hours when I can and she's happy enough because she knows she gets plenty for her money."

Betty was only seventeen years older than me. Life for her had been physically hard, but she always had time for others. She hadn't any interest in clothes and the fripperies of life, and she certainly hadn't time for courting. Somebody somewhere was missing out because she was a rare gem who gave everything while expecting nothing in return.

"I can give your mam her lunch, so why not take the opportunity to put your feet up?" she asked me, brushing my hair from my face. She smelled of clean, honest soap and I thought of Freddie.

I looked down, touched by her tenderness, the small gestures affecting us the most when we're running on empty.

But I didn't want to rest. Rest gave me time to think, rest gave me time to worry. I nodded to placate her and not rebuke her kindness.

"I nearly forget to mention," Betty said over her shoulder on the way to the kitchenette in the corner, "Mrs Cooper was asking after you. She said she hoped your mam was on the mend and sends her regards."

My stomach twisted when I recalled the conversation with Edward in the moonlight before he left on Christmas Eve.

I watched Betty slicing ham with the skill of someone who had done it daily for years—not too thick nor too thin.

Mrs Cooper was not a name I wanted to hear. I considered my response and the correct pitch of my voice, deciding to err on the side of caution and be concise. I tried to quash the unpleasant memory of only seconds before.

"How kind of her," I muttered.

"Well, there's none so kinder than her as we know. We chatted a while and between you and me I asked if Mr Cooper was alright. I can't put my finger on it I told her, but he doesn't look himself. She said he had work trouble but typical man, he won't talk to her about it. I don't know, Miss Delfina, rich or poor, we all take it in turns to have our problems to deal with."

Shaking her head, she lit the gas stove with a match to warm my mother's soup.

Edward had been playing with fire too long. I had a trump card up my sleeve, and it looked as though I was going to have to use it, but how?

We looked as bad as each other and I worried people might put two and two together and get the wrong answer before long. How ludicrous he still spent each night outside my home. He needed to grow up as I had because my family needed me as his family needed him. He should stay home of an evening and not moon after someone who was out of reach. Edward needed to be a husband and, if this was out of the question, he should at least be a father.

After Betty left, my mother took her usual nap, and I took a walk around the awakening garden. Stopping at the yew tree, I ran my finger over the thick, gnarled trunk Edward will have touched hundreds of times before. I wonder if it was the tree that brought about my sudden epiphany as I finally thought of a course of action. Checking my watch, I knew I should strike whilst the iron was hot, so I didn't lose my nerve.

I ran inside to Freddie's study and sat in the leather captain's chair, scrabbling for a notepad in the desk drawers. Finding a pad in the bottom drawer, I dipped the nib of the fountain pen in the black inkwell then stopped with it in mid-air, poised to write. I hadn't given any thought to the content, but the short note could have unknown repercussions. I considered some of them then cast them aside. I must write the letter I decided.

"Mr Cooper," I wrote, then stopped, looking up to stare into the eyes of my grandfather's portrait above the fireplace, "I would be most grateful if you could meet me at the brewery office at midday tomorrow, as we have some furniture which may be of use to the school. I thank you in advance and I shall be there regardless so please do not worry if this date or time is inconvenient, and I shall contact you again to rearrange. Sincerely, Mrs Braithwaite-Walker."

Folding the crisp note, I placed it in a sealed envelope, writing Mr Cooper on the front in capital letters, thinking this would make the handwriting more non-descript if it fell into the wrong hands. The content of the note was innocent enough should this be the case.

I had an hour to wait but although I was nervous, I wasn't deliberating. At just after four o'clock, knowing Edward would be leaving work, I headed in the direction of the village school. I counselled myself to slow my pace, so it seemed as though I was only taking an afternoon stroll.

He saw me at the very moment I saw him. I watched as he struggled to hide his muddled emotions, his shock, delight, confusion. There was nobody around in the street, but we had to proceed with the utmost caution in case anyone appeared. That day was Friday and the following day being Saturday meant Freddie would be at *The Raven* for his one and only drinking session of the week. Even he could see we no longer had the funds for him to go out drinking beer every evening. Saturdays were by then his only reprieve from the grim reality we were living in.

My conversation with Edward on the street was brief and banal but it served the purpose of being able to surreptitiously press the note into his hand.

I then walked on, my breathing gradually returning to normal, relieved my mission was a success.

*

I stop talking to the old woman now to relive that moment with Edward on the street, and the compulsion which drove me to take such measures. She sees it as a sign, an indication we are to take a break from our discussion. Shuffling towards the window, she relights the burnt-out lantern at the window. We'd been sitting in almost complete darkness, other than the lowering light from the fire for some time.

She settles herself back in her chair, eyes questioning me over a sudden thought I can see has occurred to her.

"Have you told me yet of the terrible thing that happened?" she enquired.

I turn to stare at the fire now with a distressing recollection of the memory, the memory of the terrible thing.

Shaking my head in response, I try to free myself from the remorse it rekindles. We know I've told her many terrible things already.

I sigh.

"I really wish that I had," I say.

Chapter 19

My office looks as though I left to nip out except it's been three days since I was last here.

Over the years I've made my room a cosy home from home, everything neatly to hand so the brewery administration can run like clockwork. Perhaps could run like clockwork would be more apt now. For what good it does me, I sometimes think Miss Porter would be proud of her prodigy.

I still come into work just not very often and the way things are heading, not for much longer. How I miss it. I think about my father driving me reluctantly to work that first Monday when I was eighteen. He'll be turning in his grave now at the thought of his life's work going to wrack and ruin.

Freddie told me yesterday evening the last vestige of hope—the hope *Bass* might buy us out—has disappeared. After encouraging signs they've now seen the books and realised how parlous the finances are. They can just wait for us to wither on the vine and then buy up the equipment and tenanted houses at rock-bottom prices. We're simply no longer a going concern and keeping what they see as a small brewery afloat has no interest to them. Even the Braithwaite brand doesn't seem to count for anything. The once high and mighty Braithwaite's brewery will soon be having its bones picked over. Freddie and I have long since given up pointless banalities such as, "Don't worry, we'll sort it out," or, "Something will turn up."

Now we must look for work. If we could both secure something full-time, we might survive but even then, I doubt we would be able to cover the cost of heating the hall alone. I'm in denial from the doctor's prognosis, but I long for my mother's health to improve enough so we can at least consider selling and moving into somewhere more affordable. Despite Betty's best efforts to feed me, my mother is top of the list of serious concerns which are culling my appetite, turning me into a living, walking ghost of my old self.

I must put these concerns in a box for later though because the conversation which awaits is more pressing. I must focus and do everything in my power to make Edward see sense because woe betide if Freddie comes across him in the grounds. I hope my trump card will sway him in my one last-ditch attempt. Short of going to the police and risk a public scandal, this is all I can think to do. Regardless, all the police would be able to do is have a quiet word as no crime has been committed.

Glancing out of the window I see Edward approaching on his bike, his fair hair flowing back from his face making it appear pinched and sallow. His expression gives nothing away because he has no indication of what's afoot. For once I'm in the driving seat and he's a willing passenger, no doubt keen to know where we're heading together. I swallow my heart back down at the thought.

He heads towards the brewery entrance, and I watch him through the glass doors as he dismounts his bike then leans it against the wall alongside my own. Now the weather has improved, I've taken to using a bike, but Freddie still drives to work. I enjoy the freedom hopping onto a bike brings though I've kept my mother in the dark about it. I imagine the horror on her face should she discover her daughter has lowered herself enough to pedal around the neighbourhood for all and sundry to see.

Freddie travels here in the last of my father's collection of cars, until he sells it at a significant discount like the others. I'm convinced the buyers can smell our desperation before they even begin to haggle. I think of the days when Freddie and I drove to work in the Morris, full of animated discussions about how we could save the brewery. Full of hope.

Edward smiles at me now as I beckon him inside. Though I'm certain nobody would ever turn up on a Saturday afternoon, I still lock the doors.

"This way," I say.

I catch his eye and look away quickly then lead him up the stairs to the carpeted corridor with my eyes forward. I don't want to encourage him or give the impression I've arranged this meeting to plan a way forward for us.

My office is smaller, but I think it only right we should be on my territory. I try to close my mind to any thoughts of Freddie and my father though it's a struggle. My mouth is dry with anticipation for what lays ahead. I allow myself just one hour as I'm keen not to leave my mother alone for any longer.

I nod to the chair I've placed on the other side of my desk, ensuring there is a physical barrier between us. I also hope it might serve as an emotional barrier for him. He glances at the chair, his smile no longer anywhere to be seen, then his eyes return to stare at me. He will have many questions.

Folding my oldest dress under me I sit down and keep my hands under the desk to hide the fact they are shaking. I was determined not to dress to impress in any way and give false hope. Edward sits down opposite me, his glazed eyes making him seem in a stupor.

As I breathe deeply, my head swims so the outline of his face becomes blurred.

"Well, I must start by apologising for being so evasive about the reason I needed to speak with you, but I'm sure you realise I had no alternative. Although the matter is pressing, this discussion will not be one you predicted."

Over the last twenty-four hours I've rehearsed time and time again what I want to say to him. As with every other conversation we've had, time constraints mean I can't dilly dally. This time

I can only hope he won't interrupt me and will finally listen properly to what I say.

His pallor is one of a sick man, but he is just that, a lovesick man. Knotting my hands under my thighs in the chair to secure them, the rest of my body starts to quiver. and I've lost my sense of bravado.

"Why have you summoned me here then?" he asks.

"I asked you to meet me here as this was the only place I could think of where we would not risk being disturbed."

I see fleeting hope in his eyes. I must quickly quash it.

"I also wanted to give you this."

I slide his grandmother's beautiful sapphire and diamond broach across the desk, and he stares at it then at me. He puts a hand to his mouth no doubt recalling the day he gave it to me, that fateful Christmas so many years ago. I must return the piece to its rightful owner as the broach is a family treasure.

"Edward, this is the last time I will ever meet with you. We must move on with our separate lives. We must move on for our own sake but mostly for the sake of our families. So much has changed since Christmas. You'll be aware of most of it as Betty tells me the villagers are up to speed with the state of the business. But the business worries are only part of my problem. My marriage is in tatters and my mother is, is…"

I can't bring myself to say the word because it would sound too brutal, too final. Lowering my eyes, I swallow hard. I raise my palm when I hear him draw breath to speak. I must keep going undeterred.

"Betty has noticed you're not yourself and raised it with Susanna, but I doubt your wife needed this pointing out to her. I can relate to her pain only too well as I'm suffering the same distance between myself and Freddie but for different reasons. Life has changed and we must face the real world and the people who are relying on us. The situation must end this very day, this very moment."

My lips trembling, I can't bring myself to raise my head and witness the reaction to my words. He doesn't speak.

I must continue as I will not have convinced him.

"Believe me, I know this is painful, and I know you don't want to hear it, but I love my husband. You may not love your wife, but you will certainly love your son. This deception cannot continue … and if you persist, you will leave me with no alternative but to tell your wife about your obsession. I'm sure neither of us want this to happen for her sake. I've asked you to stop too many times, and it falls on deaf ears, so I can think of nothing else to do."

I sound far stronger than I am. My emotions are just below the surface ready for me to reveal them should he continue with his pleading. I can't take anymore.

I soon forget them when I hear a strange noise. A loud laugh pierces the silence of the brewery and I instantly raise my head, somehow disturbed by the sinister sound. Surely such a laugh would never escape Edward.

I stare wide-eyed with bewilderment, feeling something new, instinctive … I feel fear. I'm struggling to recognise him, his face is a grotesque mask, unidentifiable as the man who has only looked at me before with tenderness.

"So, you finally get to the point about why you've lured me here and under false pretences no less. You're done with me, Effie and you want to forget me, to resume our former lives. Am I right in thinking also you would prefer us to pretend nothing ever happened between us?"

The question is rhetorical, his tone of voice chilling. The Edward of old has left and swiftly. His sarcasm is unsettling and now I'm not sure if I will be able to explain myself adequately or if he will even listen to reason.

"Edward, this conversation is upsetting for me," I say, "I only want you to stop before somebody discovers what you are doing and why. I may or may not have loved you, but that was a long time ago, another life.

Although I'm trying to console him, my voice has lost some of its assuredness. This reaction is not the one I was expecting from him. I was expecting resistance but not resistance in such a manner.

"It's too late for that, Effie, it's too late for the redemption you talk about. It will be impossible to revert to my old life and forget you; going back is no longer an option for me. I've lived in hope too long. I've done plenty of thinking since Christmas and I can't allow you to cast me aside now you consider me surplus to requirements. I refuse to go back home to live a dull life with a dull wife. I won't do it I tell you."

"Edward," I say, affected now by this new persona, "I find it completely unacceptable to speak to me this way. You've always had the option to escape if you wanted to, even without me."

His face now has the strangest expression.

"I must say, your unpleasant manner has taken me by surprise."

The next thing I see is Edward lunging around the desk, his face now almost touching my own. His expression is menacing, full of fury. I slide downwards in my chair to try to escape but I'm not quick enough. He grabs me roughly by my arms, pulling me towards him. I panic as I struggle to free myself from his grip.

"Please let go of me Edward, you're scaring me now. I never thought you would treat me this way. You said you loved me, but this is not love."

His breath is far too hot and too close for comfort.

"You stupid girl!" he shouts, his mouth so near to my ear the volume is painful, "I'm not some perfectly penned hero from one of your novels, Freddie's not the villain of the piece. We're just two men, madly in love with you, so much so you're steadily driving us to insanity. What do you know of me, Effie? What do you truly know of me other than what you've gleaned from a few home tuition sessions and one brief, interrupted kiss? Everything you think you know is in your girlish dreams, your fantasies. You may have been a foolish child, but you knew the power you wielded and what it still does to me and to Freddie."

As he pulls me towards him, I raise my knee and push it forward with such force his arms drop, and he doubles over. I lift my skirts to flee but he grabs me before I can leave the room, and I reach for anything to hand. The anything turns out to be an iron letter sealer. Many an hour I'd used it to seal our letters with wax imprinted with the Braithwaite's company stamp. It gives our correspondence a touch of class.

I swing it towards Edward, and it allows me to make my escape from his clutches and down the stairs. I fumble with the front door bolt until I'm overcome with relief when I feel it slide open. Grabbing my bike, I jump aboard and pedal furiously, my chest tight with fear.

I left my poor mother far longer than the anticipated hour in the end.

As I neared the village, I knew I needed to pull myself together quickly. Weaving through the streets, each corner I turned I checked I was alone before heading down on my bicycle because I couldn't risk running into anyone.

All the time I was thinking of him, I couldn't even bear to think his name by then, and I knew he had hit the nail on the head about one thing during his damning assessment of my character. I would have realised it if only I'd put my romantic daydreams to one side for a moment: he had never been anything other than a stranger, an acquaintance at best. How could I have loved him when I didn't know the first thing about him or his true nature?

Traumatised, I was far too distracted then to notice somebody was watching me.

But for once, on that occasion at least it wasn't Edward Cooper.

Chapter 20

The old woman's eyes hold mine.

They're brimming with compassion but as I watch her throat move, her shoulders rise slightly, I can see she is losing her composure.

"You were unwise in your choice of meeting place," she says. "However, I think you have forgotten one crucial factor: Edward was entirely responsible for his actions, and you were entirely the innocent party. It would serve you well to ponder this a moment before we continue."

She takes me unawares as I have never considered this before. I have since regretted arranging the meeting with Edward, and I was woefully unprepared for the turn of events.

But taking drastic measures was all I had left by then. I still believe to this day he would *never* have left me alone of his own accord otherwise.

What bothers me most of all is that he told me I was aware of the affect I had on him as though I enjoyed it. That certainly wasn't the case, his obsession only terrified me.

The woman's eyes are upon me as I reflect.

I was pleased when I caught the attention of the opposite sex as a young girl. When suddenly you become noticed, you enjoy the feeling. I doubt I'm alone in this.

However, since then, I've been too involved with the demands of life. My father's death, a failing family business, a husband who was set on pushing me away and a sick mother left me with little time for vanity.

My intention in meeting with Edward was honourable. I arranged the meeting to communicate, to reason with him though my plans went awry.

Do the old woman's words mean I may be brave enough now to consider a new verdict, one that has been too long in coming: Have I judged myself too harshly? I didn't question Edward's words and oh, how they have damaged me.

She continues to watch me intently as my mind deliberates.

"You thought you loved Edward," she tells me, almost wringing her hands in desperation to make her point, "you had an isolated childhood and reading crammed your head full of romance from a young, impressionable age. I can understand why you would think you loved him."

She understands. She understands what it meant to live a life where you were constantly alone with parents within arm's reach yet far away. It was almost as though they had abandoned me.

The woman knows I wished to race ahead to adulthood so I could make my own way and find the love I craved from someone. She consoles me.

Another person can empathise with why my loneliness drove me to make my decisions and for the first time, I feel I'm not entirely to blame. Oh, the relief—it is profound. My heart begins to stir, to come alive and sing a quiet song of liberation.

I know she hears it though she says nothing.

"Who was watching you that day?" she asks me now.

My liberty was short-lived it seems. The worst is yet to come, and I wonder how I can bear to relive it. But what would be the point in turning back now? I don't even think that I could.

I shuffle position in my chair and bow my head, preparing myself for the emotional ride ahead.

*

"On my return to the hall I put my bike in the shed. I was keen to see my mother, but I needed to tidy myself beforehand.

So, you can imagine my shock and surprise when after opening the front door the sight of Freddie greeted me in the hallway. He was back early from the pub, waiting with a strange look on his face. I almost dropped my hat and bag on the old settle and stared at him, as though my husband was the last person I would expect to see in my home. I was struck mute, unsure how to handle his untimely reappearance.

Swaying slightly, he reached for the banister to steady himself. The sudden movement made me take a step backwards, certain he had found out my secret and was going to strike me. I know now, this would never have been the case.

His expression changed to a look of horror at the realisation then his face softened as he studied me a moment. He noticed my slightly unkempt appearance.

"My love, you don't look yourself. What on earth has happened?"

Sweet, kind words threw my thoughts asunder. A swathe of guilt coddled itself tightly around me. I struggled to respond as I had become so unused to him showing concern for my welfare.

"I…I fell off my bike and I'm shaken is all. I wasn't expecting you home at this hour."

He strode quickly over, placing an arm around my shoulder to guide me upstairs.

"Come now, you must wash your face and change. Your mother was asking for you and we wouldn't want to alarm her."

The knot in my stomach lessened as I leaned into him. Freddie would always protect me from harm. I was safe and sound once more.

I glanced up at my husband and he stared down at me as we walked up the stairs together as if we did it all the time. If it could be possible, he seemed almost sobered in a few short minutes, and I remember thinking it was the most we'd spoken to each other in months. I couldn't comprehend why he'd left the pub before closing time and why he was being so attentive.

In the end I only had to wait a little while longer to find out the answers to both those questions.

Every night still Edward maintained his vigil. The sight was more than unsettling. I was terrified when I drew the curtains each evening by then. Why would he want to continue with his pursuit of me when things ended so badly between us? Power was the only answer.

Thankfully, Freddie was home more and not just because we couldn't afford for him to drink at the pub. He appeared to want to be at home to be near me. He was communicative, even making plans for life after Braithwaite's.

"I think I'll see if the mill has any vacancies to buy us some time," he told me one morning at breakfast, "something is better than nothing and I think my pride will just about stand it. Assuming they will take me back."

He managed a half-smile then leaning across the table, he covered his hand with my own. I knew what he was referring to in buying us some time. My mother was getting weaker by the day and hope was fading fast. I was finally starting to accept that the worst might happen soon. Being able to sell the hall was no consolation.

I was so relieved by Freddie's change of heart. Relieved and grateful we had each other to lean on. Sometimes, I could almost forget about that horrible day for a moment.

But a failing mother and bankruptcy weren't the only life-changing events looming.

I was pregnant.

The moment I'd been waiting for since we married had been confirmed two days previously by the doctor. I should have been elated, telling Freddie, then perhaps running to tell Janet the news we'd prayed would happen for so many years. We could laugh about the silliness of Christmas Eve and make plans for having young babies together with them growing up the best of friends.

But I couldn't do any of those things. I couldn't because I wouldn't allow myself to believe a baby would survive such turmoil. The distress would crush me if the worst happened, so it was better to deny the reality for a while at least.

*

The woman waits for me to continue silently, patiently. The pain from the cold memory is making it difficult to breathe and I grab my chest. I wait a moment before I continue, fighting the urge to stop talking.

I must face this memory head on, we have no other way to move forward. I dig deep inside me to find the strength.

*

"The following night Freddie came home and told me Pawson's had sent him away with a flea in his ear. They still held a grudge about him leaving them years before and they wouldn't budge, he said. They were more than happy to sit by and enjoy watching the vulture's circling Braithwaite's. The encounter must have been brutal for a proud man such as Freddie, but I was proud of him. He bit the bullet and did it for us.

"We'll have to think further afield, Effie but without a car I think our options are limited."

I wanted to offer to find work myself, but in my condition, I no longer had that option. I couldn't find any words to console him, making me feel useless and inadequate. Weary, I wanted to go to bed and put an end to the day. We had the same thoughts on the matter, deciding an early night might be just what we needed.

When I looked out of the window, thankfully Edward was nowhere in sight. Oh, thank heavens, he's finally seen sense, I thought then made my way upstairs close on Freddie's heels.

I went to the top floor as always to check on mother. I spent a good part of the day up there by then. She liked the room to be kept warm and the stuffy air made it difficult to bear in pregnancy.

I found her in a deep induced sleep. She hadn't moved since the last time I'd checked on her, and I put my face to hers to be sure she was still breathing. I stared down at the pathetic sight of her on the bed, a shadow of her former self. That person was long gone, but the shadow was still clinging on.

Leaving my mother, I went down the attic steps to join Freddie in our bedroom.

I thought of the baby. My marriage was undoubtedly in a different place, but we'd been taking life day by day and I still wanted this to continue for a while.

I decided such thoughts would have to keep for another time, as I climbed into bed exhausted. I fell asleep to the rhythmical sound of Freddie's breathing, his arms wrapped tightly around me. The solace of a good night's sleep was much needed.

I hardly seemed to have closed my eyes when we both awoke with a start at an urgent hammering on the front door. Panicking, I checked the clock at the side of the bed, surprised to find it was still only just before midnight.

Freddie, still bleary-eyed, jumped up to put on his dressing gown, flashing me a concerned look as the banging continued relentlessly. He told me to stay where I was but once he'd left the room, I jumped up and followed him, pausing at the top of the stairs.

He had barely had a chance to unlock the doors and turn the handle when he fell backwards towards the wall. I screamed at the sight, then I remember shouting his name. The silhouette of a man practically filled the doorway, confirming my suspicions before I even heard his voice or saw his face.

"Go get her!" he yelled, shrugging off Freddie who was trying to pull him back by the shoulder, "Get her down here now! I'm sick of it."

"Have you lost your mind?" Freddie shouted, shutting the door, "Get the hell out of my house!" His face was white with shock.

Wrapping my robe tighter around me I tried to get a better view.

"I've told my wife and now I'm telling you. You'll not stand in my way of having her. She was happy enough to have me when it suited her, now the time has come for me to suit myself."

Freddie moved deftly sideways to block the bottom of the stairs just as Edward saw me on the landing above.

"Now look here," Freddie said, "this is neither the time nor the place to discuss it. Coming to our home and scaring us half to death in the dead of night. Get back to your own home and your own family."

His last sentence was composed, but I knew well enough about my husband's temper when pushed to suddenly be concerned for both of them. But Edward was oblivious, the remark going right over his head.

I recall wondering briefly if Edward was drunk, right before I watched him catch Freddie off guard, punching him twice, first in the eye then full on his nose. He was like a crazed madman.

Freddie crashed to the floor, knocking a lamp off the hallway table on his way down. In a panic I ran down the stairs, jumping onto Edward's back, clawing his face from behind. I gave no thought whatsoever to anything, all I cared about was protecting Freddie. He was powerful and Edward no match for him. I briefly recalled the scene in the alleyway all those years before. Thomas Baker had been very lucky he was full of drink at the time and Freddie was too honourable to take advantage.

Freddie rose from the floor, his hand touching his nose in a look of disbelief that Edward could knock him down. But it was quickly followed by a look that filled me with dread.

Edward had caught him off balance, but Freddie was more than capable of taking a punch. I only knew I needed to try to intervene.

But I wasn't quick enough. As Edward attempted another punch Freddie grabbed his fist mid-swing and held onto it tightly. Edward's eyes widened as he realised what and who he was up against, yet still he wouldn't stop.

In a flurry of flailing fists Freddie delivered a final punch to Edward's jaw. He fell to his knees and then dropped to lay motionless on the ground.

Freddie was still watching over Edward waiting for him to get up. I grabbed his dressing gown cord with both hands from behind and pulled it with all the strength I could muster.

"Enough Freddie, enough, I beg you. I know you didn't start it, but you'll swing if you don't stop yourself this very second. Please!" I shouted.

His arms went limp and then he crumpled downwards onto the bottom step, his head dropping forward to land in his hands. I knelt at his feet with my hands on his thighs.

"Oh, Freddie, I'm so sorry to have dragged you into all this. I know words can never be enough but I'm so dreadfully sorry I met him."

I spoke earnestly, but I was fearful of his next words. I had to face what he threw at me but most of all, I wanted him to still want me. I couldn't think of a life without him.

Raising his head, Freddie looked me straight in the eye. I continued waiting, unable to look away though the disgrace tormented me.

He grabbed my face between his palms.

"And so am I," he said.

He shook his head, moving his lips in a struggle to find the words.

"It pains me now to admit this, but Larry saw you that day at the brewery. He was curious why you would be going in that day. He watched you cycle there and then Cooper arrive not long after. Then he came to the pub to tell me because he couldn't stand the thought of me being made a fool of, is what he said. We haven't spoken of it since."

Tears clouded my vision as I stared at my dear husband. I shook my head. How could he want to turn a blind eye, what on god's green earth would possess him to do such a thing?

Freddie dropped his hands from my face and grabbed both of my hands with his own.

"Why couldn't Cooper just have left us alone?" his pitiful wail startled me, "I would have been able to pretend it never happened. I could have lived the lie with you forever, that you just fell off your bike. I could have buried my head so deeply in the sand and lived my life blissfully blinded to the cold light of day to … to the bitter end."

I watched tears drop from his chin to settle on the hairs of his chest, the phrase, the bitter end echoing around my mind. He was prepared to live the lie evermore just to have me.

"It was one kiss in a weak moment years ago when he tutored me. I've been trying to get away from his clutches, his obsession with me since then. That's why I met him at the brewery, to let him know if he didn't stop, I would have no alternative but to tell his wife. I don't know if I could have done, but it was all I had left. Please, believe me, Freddie, I love *you*!"

A loud banging on the door wrenched us from our conversation.

"Police, open the door, now!"

I heard the familiar voice of Constable Stratton. Someone from the village must have heard the shouting and raised the alarm.

Panicked, I pulled my hands from Freddie's grasp and ran as fast as I could manage upstairs to the bathroom.

There on my knees on the freezing tiled floor, I retched up the acrid taste of my terrible guilt.

Chapter 21

So, now the time has come. I must stand tall and face our fate.

A sergeant came to the house and questioned me the following morning and I relived every detail of what had happened over the last few months.

He advised me Edward was in hospital and had already made a full statement accusing Freddie of an unprovoked attack. The police have arrested Freddie and charged him with assault. They interviewed us separately at the police station, and yet again Freddie protected my honour in not disclosing my connection with Edward. I know because the sergeant looked surprised when I told him. I had to tell him; I had to because Freddie was saying nothing about the incident, and I desperately wanted him to make bail. How we would find the money, set at fifty pounds, was a different worry.

So, I explained to the sergeant how Edward had attacked me and stalked me, and this led to the fight, but when the sergeant asked if there were witnesses to support my story, I realised it was a waste of time revisiting the trauma. It was little consolation that the sergeant believed me. I knew he did because he changed his manner towards me.

He will no doubt have seen enough liars in his interview room to know when someone is telling the truth.

The facts I know have been gleaned third hand either overheard or otherwise, because I haven't seen Freddie since he was led away in handcuffs to the police car. He was unable to look at me after the confession he made to me on the stairs at home.

"If you ask me," Betty says, "you've no choice in the matter. Freddie needs bail, you need money for his bail, but your mother doesn't need her pearls. Some decisions aren't really decisions at all. You can't bother her about all this, and she hasn't any need for them any longer. In any case, the pearls will be yours," she swallows, "soon enough."

I'm perching on the edge of my bed in a bedroom where I haven't slept for days. Betty's sits on the dressing table chair by the window, the sun pouring in and around her making her appear ethereal, like an angel of mercy. That's exactly what Betty is; what she's always been to me. She has a knack of administering a healthy dose of common sense just when you need it most.

I push my hair from my face, closing my eyes to reality.

"Oh, Betty, thank you for always somehow saying the right thing at the right time."

Her face pink, she gets to her feet and starts to shoo me from the room.

"Off you go, there's no time to waste if you're going to catch the train to Leeds later. You've plenty to do and so have I."

She smiles and touches my cheek and I raise a smile in return the best I can. She's always clucking, fretting about me and I always try to keep this to a minimum. This time it's proving difficult.

I make my way up to my mother in her attic rooms. I hope she'll be sleeping so I can just quietly slip in and then out without a word.

The quote, "Oh what a tangled web we weave, when first we practice to deceive," floats around my head. One lie begets another, then on and on the web grows, to choke you with its misery.

My mother's fast asleep in one of her many bed jackets. This one is of turquoise with yellow flowers embroidered on the collar. It makes her look old. She's never disclosed her age to me or anyone else I wouldn't imagine but I think she must only be in her mid-fifties. Her appearance isn't helped by her thick now grey hair being freshly combed in a tidy but unflattering style by Betty. Her head is resting on a mountain of pillows, slightly leaning to one side and even in sleep she looks in pain. She should be in a nursing home, but she won't leave the hall, so the doctor comes and goes regularly. This will be another bill to settle before too long. She's so lucky to have Betty because our angel of mercy is the only thing that stands between my mother being able to stay at home or end her days in a state nursing home. Lack of funds would prevent her from having the best private care she would expect, and she told me she could never allow me to provide personal care.

I know where my mother keeps the pearls as she was once a creature of order and habit. I'm sure she will keep them in the same place. I cross to the walk-in wardrobe on the other side of the room, my eyes peering constantly in my mother's direction. The space she was so keen to create for herself is elegant, and I can see why until the last few months she's enjoyed living up here. Before she was ill, she was trapped, yet where would she have gone to visit if she'd been well enough to leave the house.

I pick the box from the drawer and open the lid to run my fingers over the three rows of pearls. Each gem shimmers even in the darkened wardrobe and I picture my mother clutching the pearls when agitated. I don't think I ever saw her without them, they were almost like part of her being.

I think of Betty's words and my husband's expression as he bared his soul to me. I must get out of this bedroom. I want to race far from my thoughts, knowing full well wherever I run they will stay with me. I have no escape.

Looking over my shoulder, I'm startled when my mother suddenly opens her eyes. I watch the eyrie sight as her eyes roam immediately to my face and then to the box in one swift action. She wakes so rarely nowadays, but I'm now hot under the spotlight, caught red-handed.

"I'm sorry, mother," I say.

My face is burning, and I can't find a suitable excuse.

Walking backwards I'm eager to return the pearls to their rightful place. Bail is no longer an option for Freddie, and I will just have to accept it.

"Wait," she says now, her voice breaking on the word.

I stand perfectly still in the overbearing room. I hear a bird singing above us on the roof, enjoying the warm day outside. The familiar outdoor sound provides a grim contrast to the unfamiliar situation I'm in within these walls.

She doesn't move, even lift her head from the pillow.

"Why must you take my pearls before they are yours? I know you're not a thief, Delfina."

I look at the box then down at my feet, surprised at hearing my name come from her lips after so long. I can't possibly tell her the whole truth, she's not strong enough, but I must at least confess some of it. My mother is not a fool.

"Don't lie to me."

I raise my eyes from the floor and look directly into hers.

"Freddie's in trouble."

The answer is enough but not too much.

"Are things really so bad?" she asks levelly.

This is a veiled nod to the fact she knows more about our life downstairs than we realised. I hoped we'd managed to protect her, to keep her safely away from reality up here.

Her question has hidden meaning; I must be careful how I answer.

"Things are…redeemable but only if I take action this very day."

Witnessing the small, painful movement of her adjusting her head on her pillow makes me rush towards the bed. I sit at her side and take her icy hand in mine, half-expecting her to pull away from me but she doesn't.

Coughing, she puts the handkerchief clutched in her palm to her mouth. I hand her the tumbler of water on her bedside table to drink, lifting her head tenderly. After just a sip she lays back on the pillow, visibly exhausted. She takes a laboured breath then stares beyond me.

"Well then, take action, you must," she says, with unexpected conviction, "I know some of what you've tried so hard to shield from me. I have eyes and ears… I'm frail of body, not mind. I'm not a fool."

I smile gently, recalling my description of her only seconds ago.

"No mother, you're certainly nobody's fool."

She moves her hand to rest it on my arm. I look into her watery blue eyes, taken aback then touched by such a small yet intimate gesture.

"Not in every way at least, perhaps I may have been in some."

What can she mean, I wonder? I stay quiet hoping this will encourage her to go on as the opportunities to speak to her are lessening by the day. The silence engulfs us a while, but oddly I'm not uncomfortable with it.

Her eyes roll upwards towards the ceiling. That view I realise now has been her only glimpse of the world night and day for so long.

"I've been laying here with only my thoughts for many a month, unable to read or do anything to distract me from them. I wonder if I would ever have started this conversation without dire circumstances forcing me, but I know the answer. I know I have been very foolish… in making you pay for my own dissatisfaction with life."

The change in her tone startles me more than the confession. She has her eyes fixed firmly on the ceiling unable I think to bring herself to look at me. I wonder if she's embarrassed or ashamed, or both.

"You know well enough that my list of resentment is long. I resented my dull life, my disappointing husband—I apologise as I know he was your father—my sense of isolation which I realised too late I enforced upon myself," she pauses, "worst of all has been my resentment towards you, my daughter, my only child. I resented you for being born in a different time, and because life blessed you with opportunities you appeared indifferent towards, ones which fell short for me."

I could never have expected such an admission. I'm wrong-footed by such an explosion of sentimental emotion from a mother who has shown very little. Staring at her profile I think of her words. Alongside jealousy, resentment is the most corrosive of emotions.

"I think you may be referring to the fact I am more my husband's equal in marriage. Even before then, resentful of me wanting to throw my opportunities away for fanciful love or even worse, only the idea of it?"

Turning her face my way, she smiles weakly, a wry look of humour in her expression and more than a hint of affection. It warms my heart so much that I want to cry.

"So, it seems you *were* paying attention after all. I should have given you more credit," she says.

I return her smile, gently squeezing her hand on my arm.

"I've been harsh Delfina, I know now, hard on you even. I've been jealous of you, and this never brings out the best in a person. I admit I've always thought I was above most people, even people who didn't deserve to be looked down upon. My father worked hard for his family. He wanted us to have everything he didn't have but then he indulged me, spoiled me in the literal sense. My brother was treated differently before he died which isn't unusual in families. I was my father's little princess, and he thought your father was the perfect match for me because he was like him regarding business. I thought my father had forced me to marry him but really, I could have questioned his judgment at any time. He would have listened to me because my happiness was important to him. I didn't question it however, because I had no idea about romantic feelings. Worse, at the age I am, I still don't have any idea. I'm disappointed with myself now for looking down on your father when, certainly in the beginning, he only ever wanted the business to flourish so I could continue to live in the style I was accustomed."

Her words are flowing freely when only moments ago she was the stranger she always has been. But I should imagine the thought of impending death unshackles your mind and your tongue.

"You know, not all the trouble we're in is down to the success of our competition."

My eyebrows raise. My mother knows so much and apparently, she's keen to share it while she can.

"What do you mean?" I ask.

My stomach tightens; I'm curious, but not completely sure I want to be enlightened.

"Well, I suppose as I'm being candid, I may as well continue in the same vein. I'm sure you will be surprised to discover that years ago a member of staff at the brewery had been embezzling a great sum of money for quite some time. It might also surprise you your father turned a blind eye to the deception."

My eyebrows pull together and I shake my head.

"Why would father do such a thing? It seems so out of character."

He was a businessman through and through—no time to beat about the bush with sentimentality, except perhaps with me.

"The person in question was a valued and trusted employee who wasn't taking the money out of badness. They were taking it because they needed the money, they were desperate... and afraid."

"Do I know this person?" I ask.

"You do indeed, it was Bridget Porter, your father's secretary."

Bridget Porter? Miss Porter, my mentor who I looked up to and put on a pedestal.

"Her mother had taken ill," my mother confides, "and she needed money for her treatment. She raised the funds by placing fraudulent small orders for office supplies regularly over the course of two years."

Sitting back in my chair I laugh but in an ironic way. Miss Porter had always appeared whiter than white with her no-nonsense approach to her work.

"James Forrester found out about the fraud, but your father refused to take the matter to the police or even dismiss her. She'd worked for him for decades and he was disappointed she stole from him rather than turn to him for help. You can imagine I was furious when James came to see me about it. He wanted me to make your father see sense, even though at the time we could afford the loss. That was not the point James said, and I agreed. More frustratingly, I could not sway your father over the matter.

It served me well when you went to work at Braithwaite's because it secured Bridget's retirement. She was another I was burning with resentment towards, and I was terribly jealous of your father's loyalty to her. I even went as far as waiting outside the brewery on more than one occasion to challenge her, imagining her recoiling with horror and shame that her theft had been discovered. The thought gave me so much satisfaction at the time.

I'm glad now fate stepped in, and I lost my nerve. I have one less regret to stew over. Mores the pity I found out too late about the state of the business, but either way Bridget could not repay us, and the scandal … well, it wouldn't have sat well with me."

I've quickly discovered so much about my mother, only for her to become even more a stranger. Amid a warm day, I'm suddenly bitterly cold. Miss Porter has fallen from her pedestal, but then she was a desperate woman in desperate times. With no husband and children, her mother was her world.

"Look, I'm sure you must go," mother says, bringing me back to my own reality, "we can talk more when you've done what you must do. But I should tell you one last thing before you leave, my jealousy got the better of me because I know something you don't."

"What do you know?" I ask.

She sighs, and the bird continues to chirrup as I wait.

"Both Freddie and Edward Cooper love you. I may not have had the love-light shone my way, but I saw it long enough in my parents' eyes to know it when I saw it. You had two loves, when I had none, and I somehow couldn't forgive you for that."

Only a few days ago, all this would have been music to my ears after years of self-reproach. I thought I knew Miss Porter, she was almost like a mother figure, but apparently, she too was a stranger. Can we ever really know someone?

She's wrong, Edward doesn't love me, he cannot possibly love me. No love would allow someone to behave like a monster, a possessive monster. I think of Freddie locked away, alone and hopeless. I must try to make amends in whatever way I can.

My mother looks tired, but now is the time to put her straight about one thing which has prayed on my mind for years.

"I should have told you before," I say, "but I didn't think I would convince you. I was with Freddie in the alleyway that night. He was professing his love for me, nothing more, but someone made an inappropriate remark, the same man who soiled my reputation. Freddie was defending my honour. He's only ever wanted to look after me in his own troubled way. The problem is that he's never thought himself good enough for me."

Her mouth curls slightly, her expression softer than I've seen it before. If I ever picture my mother, she's immaculately dressed and taut faced, always ready to go to war over some matter be it in attack or defence.

"Oh, to have such passion surround me. I cannot even begin to contemplate."

Her tone of voice is light, free from bitterness. As I smile back at her, I stroke her fringe gently from her forehead. How can I feel self-conscious when all barriers between us have suddenly been taken away? She was brave enough to do that for us at her weakest moment. She is my mother; I am her daughter and time is running out to not give her all of me.

"Go to your husband," she whispers, "go and do everything in your power to save him."

I stare at her a moment. Should I tell her my secret I wonder, but I don't dither long.

"You're going to be a grandmother," I whisper.

My baby suddenly becomes real. I have a physical shift in me at the thunderbolt moment in my life. I am to become a mother.

A spark of something wonderful ignites behind my mother's eyes. They glisten my way and I swallow hard to compose myself.

"Do it right this time," she tells me, "Do it right for both of us."

I lean over to place a kiss on her clean cheek, as a wet tear reaches my lips. A tear of joy from her for once.

"We were both at fault, I've made mistakes and I'm paying the price, but I'm truly sorry for deceiving you with your pearls," I whisper.

I watch another tear sparkle in the sunlight streaming through the window, then drop quickly onto the pillowcase.

"They were always our pearls, Delfina," she says, "and I've come to think it for the best the necklace is removed from this house, they've done far too much damage."

Damage? I shake my head.

"Pearls are tears, so they say, and I think we've both shed enough of those. Even if they're mainly the kind of tears which silently scream to be released from the deepest place within us."

Chapter 22

My baby stirs. He or she will be waiting for me to settle so they too can nestle down for the night. I wonder again if I carry a boy or a girl.

Fatigue is doing its best to overwhelm me, and I can see my host feels the same. But neither of us want to give in to it and neither of us will, not yet.

"Did you ever see your mother again?" she asks me.

I'm unable to respond and she doesn't push for an answer. I wait a good while before I set off again on my path.

The end is in sight, but this is no encouragement to go on.

*

The magistrates accepted Freddie wasn't likely to abscond, and he made a solemn oath not to go anywhere near Edward Cooper. The case was adjourned for further police enquiries. The police made no objection to bail and when I looked across at the sergeant who had interviewed me, I'm sure I saw an almost imperceptible nod, as if my honesty had counted for something.

I somehow managed to cobble together the money for his bail fee. The pearls were nearly enough, but I also sold some jewellery of my own. I was only thankful I didn't need to include my wedding ring in the deal. We'd already been to Leeds a few times before to sell family treasures to forestall the closure of Braithwaite's. That was until we came to our senses and faced reality: It was like trying to hold dry sand in a sieve.

I waited for Freddie to return to me, pacing up and down frantically. He didn't want me to attend court, so I stayed away as the last thing I wanted was to distress him further. Though it was surreal to be waiting for my husband to return home after a court case, we had no alternative but to just get on with living our strange, new life.

Understandably, Loftus was alight with talk of the fight and other ugly rumours. I didn't know how near the truth they were, but I knew from the twitching of curtains as I passed on my bike and the way people stopped mid-conversation as I approached that we were the subject of them. Discretion was never a strong point with the villagers, and they saw no reason to pretend even at the best of times.

I'd called on Janet the day before the conversation with my mother. As I knocked on the door to her cottage, my tongue glued to the roof of my mouth, I pictured all eyes of the village upon me. I knocked again when there was no answer. I could hear Rose chatting through the open window, so I knew they were in.

We'd bumped into each other in February, after the awkwardness of Christmas Eve but it was before Larry discovered I met Edward at the brewery. We were awkward to begin with, "pussyfooting around the bleeding obvious," as Janet would have termed it once. It was humour which enriched our bond and we even shared a joke that day about me adopting Rose if I wanted a baby so badly because she was becoming a "right little madam." It was good to release the valve and address the source of the problem. I walked away with a renewed sense of hope I hadn't quite lost my best friend after all.

I was wondering if I should bother knocking again when I heard the click of the latch. Janet peered at me through the crack of the door, her expression strained and aloof. My mouth opened, but the right words eluded me at that moment. I wasn't welcome in her home any longer, what could there be to say?

"I may as well tell you now as later, Effie," she said, holding tightly to the handle as though I might attempt to kick the door in, "I'd be obliged if you wouldn't call on us again. It …it was bad enough after I found out about your connection with Edward Cooper but after all this trouble, I can't have it. Freddie and Larry are best friends, and my loyalty lies with my husband."

Her face reddened as she spoke, her words sounding as though she was reading from a script. She'd obviously thought about this conversation long and hard, more than likely had a few sleepless nights over it.

"I understand, Janet," I said, "but you must know that I wanted to discuss what was going on with you, I just had no idea how to broach the subject."

"You should have given it a try. You wanted it all, you were greedy. I know it hasn't been easy, trying for a baby an' all, and the brewery folding, but this is called marriage. It's not all sunshine and roses. I thought you were better than this Effie, I really did. To think how many times, I've defended you against gossip."

Her flat tone of voice was worse than her shouting angrily at me.

"I've been proud to call you my friend, Janet. I swear to you I'm not making excuses, but the meeting at Braithwaite's wasn't what you think. I wouldn't want to explain in the street, but a mistake as a young girl has led to all this trouble. Please don't think I'm not taking responsibility; I've tried to make things better, but they only became worse. I hope you can believe me."

She shook her head, "Not really if I'm honest, they're only words. We know how much Freddie loves you, trusted you even. But, who knows, it might be some consolation one day if we

214

see him happy again. Though this may be well into the future from what I hear."

I wanted to tell her I loved Freddie the same way he loved me. But the gap in the door was already narrowing.

Watching on as she closed the door on our friendship, I waited until she disappeared, thinking all the while she might change her mind. When she'd gone, I knew it was for good and the realisation shook me so much I was dizzy. I picked up my bike from the ground and pushed it alongside me using it almost as a crutch, too unsteady to ride. It would be a long walk of shame back to Carleton Hall.

I stopped and clutched my chest with a physical pain in my heart, it was real.

They lied; they lied when they said it's better to have loved and lost than to have never loved at all.

Oh, and what a love I'd lost in my dearest friend.

Chapter 23

We finally received word of the date of Freddie's hearing. I'd thought carefully about what to wear. It had to be black for many reasons, so I chose a swing dress with a cream collar and cuffs, so I didn't look too sombre and austere.

As I left the house, I asked Betty if she had any further news on Edward and she told me that as far as she knew he was still in hospital. Perhaps she wasn't telling the truth and didn't want to add to my worries, I couldn't be sure.

This time I refused to stay away, but I agreed to wait outside. I watched Freddie's solicitor, Mr Stapleton as he led Freddie through the solemn, heavy oak doors; he had a tense expression which I didn't like the look of one little bit.

I paced around the precinct outside oblivious to the pouring rain. It was early enough and wet enough, so only a few people were milling around. I had no idea what reaction to expect, and I was nervous to face him.

An hour passed before finally Freddie turned the corner, hands in pockets, collar up against the rain. He stopped dead in his tracks and our eyes clashed and held fast, both startled even though we were expecting to see each other. Peering through the rain at me it was as though he couldn't quite believe I was there. Did he think I'd change my mind I wondered then. We took the few steps to reunite, and I looked into the weary yet still love-filled eyes of my husband. His suit had crumpled, and his hair had fallen in curls onto his forehead, a sign of him running his hands through it with agitation. He looked so endearing.

I lifted my umbrella to shelter us, his arms curling around me in an embrace and our lips touched tentatively at first, then more intensely, fiercely even. I was oblivious to the world surrounding us, the only thought in my mind was that love is all. Love *is* all. Sometimes we bury this truth too deeply in our consciousness to remember when fear or pride take hold. They distract us, make us forget.

"You look beautiful," he told me, "I've lived this moment over and over, awake and in my dreams. You're the only one who got me through, yet still I wondered if you'd be here, right up until the moment I saw you."

I buried my face into his chest, listening to the rain and breathing the clean scent of him which lingers on the dressing gown I lay beside each night on our bed.

"I'll always be waiting," I say, my muffled voice barely coherent, "please don't ever doubt it again."

His arms tightened, and we stood awhile.

"What happened," I asked eventually, trying not to sound overly anxious.

"They're sending me up to the Assizes in Leeds. The case is too serious for the magistrates to hear," he replied, as nonchalantly as he could muster, but failing to hide the shock.

Just how badly hurt was Edward I thought and what had he said to the police?

"Oh Freddie, I'm so sorry. This is all my fault - how could I have allowed this deceitful, terrible man into our lives. I wish I'd hit him harder that night at the brewery."

Freddie smiled; "Well I don't see how that would help. It would be you in the dock and me stood out here in the rain."

I smiled weakly up at him.

"I wish we could stay away from the village, at least for a few days, but I have mother to think of. In any case, we don't have the money, so we have no alternative but to return home."

"It has to be done sooner or later, so we'd best get it over with," he said, stroking my hair.

He sighed as he took the umbrella from me and slid his arm around my shoulder to head to the train station together. We glanced at each other on the way there from time to time. How grateful we were to be able to bring about our reunion against all the odds stacked against us.

At the station, there was over an hour before the next train, and I spotted the café on the platform. It was almost empty, so we found two chairs by the window, and I settled myself while Freddie made his way to the counter. I tidied my hair and reapplied lipstick using my compact mirror. It was oddly like we were on our first date. In a way, it was the first date of our new, true relationship.

Freddie returned and set down two cups of hot sugary tea, unbuttoning his suit jacket to join me on the seat to my right. I wiped a hole in the steam building up on the windowpane with a napkin so we could watch the hustle and bustle of the platform as we sat in silence. It was as though I was dreaming as I saw the world going on as usual through the steamy window. What would become of us, what were we to do in the next moment let alone the next weeks and months ahead? I had no idea, but I had to try to focus on this moment we'd waited for to begin with.

He took my hand under the table, stroking it gently with his thumb. I could almost hear him piecing the words together in his mind. I stared through the hole in the condensation, waiting, wondering. He cleared his throat.

"I won't ask why Effie because I know the answer," he said, "I only want to know if you love him."

I whipped my head to look at him as he stared down at our entwined hands, playing with my wedding ring. The question was so direct it took my breath away. This wasn't what I was expecting him to ask, it was so bold and to the point, so unlike Freddie's evasive manner of late. I realised it was because he had to be finally rid of the painful question that had been torturing him.

He was a little boy lost, and I thought briefly then of something which should have been obvious. We were both young, no more than children roleplaying and fumbling our way through a testing adulthood. We lacked the crucial ingredient which is life experience. We had little experience of life but somehow, I'd been thinking until that very moment we should have all the answers.

Freddie was waiting for my answer and for once I was so glad to be able to put him out of his misery.

"Honestly, I imagined I was in love with him, yes. However, I barely knew him and what I did know wasn't real. He misled me into thinking he could whisk me away from the misery of home, or maybe I was blinkered by the idea of love and just couldn't see enough. Whatever it was, I know now it fell far short of love. Fate had a better love in store for me."

He raised his head to give me a shy smile as though I'd handed him a long-awaited gift. I never thought he would be tossing and turning with that worry haunting his nights away from me.

"You know, I sometimes think you're cursed, Effie. You are beautiful inside and out, but perhaps this is more of a burden than a blessing. It stirs a primal instinct in a man which he can't ignore or turn his back on. If it wasn't Cooper, it would have been someone else. I must take my share of the blame because I pushed you away and neglected you for so many years. Too many years. My pride got the better of me."

I cupped his cheek and faced the pain in his eyes head on. It was visceral. He pushed his face into my palm for a second and closed his eyes.

"We've both made mistakes, but we can't let them destroy us," I said. I sounded far braver than I felt.

"I could have coped with what I'd found out if I didn't have to think about it, tackle it," he said, "I wanted to deny it so hard to myself it ceased to be true. The warped plan I'd made served me well for a while."

His plan had worked, he had me convinced. I had a powerful urge to kiss him and try to take some of the rawness away, but I didn't want to draw attention to us, so I settled for squeezing his hand tightly in both my own instead.

I looked down at the two cold cups of tea on the table and checked my watch. We still had some time before we needed to return to reality.

"I'm not sure how we can fix this you know," he said, "we must be realistic. I could be gone from your life for … some time."

He was trying to keep his voice light, but he didn't convince me.

"I'll wait. I'll sell the hall and wait for however long until we're together again. It's you,

Freddie, it was always you, I just couldn't see the wood for the trees."

I thought of the baby and when to tell him. It was too soon, I had to be sure all was well, and I only knew it wasn't the right time or place to tell him. I simply couldn't imagine when and where that would be.

I needn't have worried so."

Chapter 24

Edward is gone.

He discharged himself from hospital and left with only the clothes on his back to his name. Betty said Susanna knows nothing of his whereabouts, so heaven knows where he is.

I'm relieved. This must surely mean he has recovered and will help Freddie's case, but any relief is tinged by the dread of him returning to cause more trouble. I must still watch my back.

So, now I need to find the strength to do the decent thing and face the other victim of this terrible situation … Susanna.

"I don't expect Susanna to see me, Betty, but I can only try. This is all I have to offer."

We're sitting in the back garden, taking in some much-needed fresh air. A stroll around the village would be better but I only venture out of the grounds when necessary. Freddie took on the role of gardener for the very same reason but also to distract his overactive mind whilst waiting for his new court date. Mr Stapleton said the missing victim complicates the situation although there is no suggestion Freddie was involved in his disappearance.

He has little to do to keep occupied but we've resigned ourselves to being prisoners when ironically, we can both come and go as we please in the village at present. Freddie has gone to Janet and Larry's house for a while after Larry passed a note to Betty. He will never set foot in the hall again and I'm persona non grata, but Larry cannot turn his back on his best friend.

My life has become a nasty little pendulum, swinging madly between the need for my mother to stay with us and the need for us to move away from the village. The conflicting thoughts which flutter around my mind of late beggar belief.

"That remains to be seen," Betty says, "but if she doesn't speak to you today, she may tomorrow or one day in the future. You must never give up hope."

Betty will be a leper in the village because of her loyalty to us I often think.

"I'm sorry you've been put in this position, Betty."

She sets her cup of tea down with a look of indignation.

"Don't you worry about me, I'm a big lass," she says, "I don't need that narrow-minded lot in the village to be judge and jury to know I'm doing the right thing. I haven't a clue about the full ins and outs of it all, but Edward Cooper took advantage of a young lass, if you ask me. They think if you have plenty of money you've no right to any problems, but they've no idea what goes on behind closed doors."

"I'll never forget your loyalty to us, I mean it. I dread to think how hard it's been for you beyond those gates."

She gets up from her seat, ready to get on and adjusts the white frill cap my mother always insisted on her wearing. She still wears it out of respect though mother wouldn't be any the wiser now.

"I'll survive, never you worry. Go on now, missy, take the high road to the schoolhouse and see what comes of it. Get it over with."

I don't need to change, only put on my hat and summer jacket because black in one form or another has been my uniform these past weeks. My stomach has started to become more noticeable, but I've been hiding it well with a trick or two.

I see Janet on the lane. She's due to have her baby any day now, and she looks ready for it to happen. Her eyes forward, I know she's trying to pretend I don't exist any longer, but I also know it will be paining her just as much as me.

Approaching the schoolhouse, I fight the urge to run back home. I pause, my hand on the gate, still unsure if I'm doing the right thing. Am I here for Susanna and Daniel or for myself to try to assuage my guilt? Both are just as prevalent, but I can't live with myself if I don't at least attempt to apologise.

I study the front door after ringing the bell and wait to see if Susanna will answer it. It's in need of a lick of paint, an indication Edward's obsession with me meant more than his family were being neglected.

The house is silent, and I wonder whether to try again. I'm somewhere between relieved and disappointed to have to delay the meeting. Perhaps there's nobody home or perhaps, like Janet, she's wondering whether to answer the door to me. I decide to leave and not force the issue.

The sound of the door handle turning makes me stop and turn around at the gate. I'm afraid of seeing Susanna in the flesh now, unsure if I can stand firm for all my good intentions. She blinks my way in the sunlight, as though she's struggling to believe her own eyes. Her pale face is almost translucent, and it won't be just from the bleaching of the sunshine.

"Well, of all the people I expected to open my door to this day, you were the last on the list."

She looks tired and older. I imagine I look the same.

"Please can I talk to you a moment?" I ask, "Only a moment, I promise I'll be gone very soon and won't bother you again."

I can see her mind working, weighing up the alternatives. I consider it a bonus for her to be engaging at all, and I don't move as I wait for her to arrive at a decision. This is a fateful one for her, for both of us.

When she gesticulates with her head for me to step inside her home, I hesitate to take the first step. Then I pick up pace to follow her and try to catch up as she heads down the hallway. I close the front door behind me and shut out the world now to be engulfed by silence.

She's out of sight and I imagine she just wants this encounter to be over with as quickly as possible. I'd be lying if I said this approach doesn't suit me well.

I've pictured Susanna and Edward in this room many times I think as I step over the threshold. I thought of them reading together, playing with Daniel on the hearth rug. Did Edward do any of this or was he too fixated with me for such trivialities? Will he ever set foot in this room again, I wonder. How I hope he's gone and gone for good, not just for a while, but Susanna may not feel the same.

She points to the chair by the fire and sits down in the chair opposite. I'm now sitting in Edwards place and feel a brief tingling sensation down my spine at the realisation.

Her blonde hair is in a neat chignon and she's wearing a navy-blue dress which looks new because of the style. She appears the epitome of elegance, bravely facing the possibility of a life of solitude for herself and her son.

Glancing at the family portraits on the mantlepiece, the windowsill, the dresser, I don't want to face what has happened, but I know I must.

I can't weather the silence any longer.

"I'm grateful to you for letting me into your home under the … circumstances. Believe me, I know nothing I say will be adequate. All I can do is try to apologise, even though I doubt you wish to hear it and I don't think for one moment I deserve the opportunity. I was unsure what to do for the best, I only knew I had to try to see you. I didn't expect to be allowed entry into your home."

I speak at a pace, almost babbling. Though my words are sincere, they still sound glib even to me and I think now I've done the wrong thing albeit in trying to do the right thing. Any words I could choose would fall short.

Devoid of emotion her eyes of hazel watch me steadily. She folds her hands in her lap, in no rush to speak and I brace myself for the onslaught. I doubt anything she said would surprise me. I've thought of everything she could throw my way, even a stinging slap.

"Effie, I would be grateful if you could do us both a favour. Take a breath, compose yourself," she says, gently.

I run my tongue over my lips, thinking I may have misheard. She sits still a moment, but my heart won't stop racing.

"First, I must ask if you know of Edward's whereabouts. I would like him to face his responsibilities."

I shake my head, surprised she's asking the obvious question.

228

"No, I'm sorry, but I would certainly tell you if I did."

The clock ticks the time away as she assesses if I'm telling the truth. She has no reason to trust me.

"So, the mystery continues," she says, "but now I've been given the opportunity, I have something to tell you and it will not be what you're expecting to hear."

I close my eyes briefly to prepare myself.

"Don't you think Edward Cooper has made us both suffer enough?"

I'm dumbfounded. I can't be certain of the meaning behind the question, so I can't think how to answer. Is she perhaps telling me she too has seen the darker side of Edward?

She interrupts the silence.

"You heard me correctly, Effie, only you and I know the man Edward really was, is. His own son is even unaware, and it will be difficult painting a picture of a saint for him when I detested his father so much."

Detested his father so much—what a thing to say. We stare at each other again and I'm not sure if seconds or minutes pass by. We're both delving around in each other's minds for answers. Slowly, steadily I understand what she's trying to say, and I see Edward's wife in an entirely different light.

The tingling down my spine returns. Oh, how unhappy she has been, and I am the only person in the world who can know just how much.

Her eyes lower as her composure finally gives way, her lower lip trembling.

"I have a confession," she says now, "I used you for my own ends, Effie. I'm not quite the embittered, betrayed wife people imagine me to be, though I've no intention of enlightening them. However, the fact remains that whilst ever Edward fixated over you, I was free."

I put my hand to my chest, shaking my head.

"We both know how unpleasant he could be, but please don't misunderstand, as much as I might like or even should stand up and say this in court on Freddie's behalf, I will not sully the reputation of my son's father. Daniel does not deserve that, and I hope you won't ask me to."

She has disclosed too much for comfort. Memories I've tried to bury for weeks have suddenly been dragged into the spotlight to be analysed, picked over. I'm feeling unsteady, unwell even.

"I would never dream of asking you to do that for us. But are you telling me you knew all along?" I ask, "Like Freddie, did you know and turn a blind eye for your own reasons?"

Her silence is a deafening confirmation.

"After he came back from the hall that night having spoken to your parents about private tuition, he was immediately changed, but I was unable to pinpoint why. As you know, I was lodging with Janet's family and working in the schoolhouse which was why I'd come to live in Loftus after we were engaged. Looking back, he never seemed in any hurry to marry but that Christmas I pushed him into setting a date for the wedding so as not to lose face. Like many a wife before me, I didn't find out his true colours until after we were married. In the end when I followed him one night to see where he went, I realised his obsession with you would quite simply let me off the hook. I wondered often whether if I hadn't had Daniel to think of if I would have returned to my parents. I'll never be sure if I would have found the courage to leave him, he has a nasty streak … as you know."

I look away blushing. How can she be certain I know of his darker side? Perhaps he spoke of the encounter at the brewery when he told her he was leaving. We both thought we knew Edward well it appears, but how wrong we were. He manipulated everyone into thinking he was a solid pillar of the community.

"I didn't want to bring a child up without a father, but it was always at the back of my mind he might leave me," she says.

I think about the moment Edward told me he could never leave Susanna, that our plans were pie in the sky. He didn't know then the depth of his feelings and how they would play out for all of us. As sure as day follows night, my memory always settles on when my mother bounced into the study to congratulate him on setting a date to be married only to discover our indiscretion. I carry this memory around with me constantly, the moment when everything began to spiral out of control.

"Over time, I worked out a way to have it all, a husband, a child, status, security and I can't lie it was working out well. The best of it was I slept in peace every night. I did manage to have it all, even if it was only for a while."

I wonder what I would have done in Susanna's shoes. Would I have found the strength to leave him? I'll never know but she worked out a way to cope with life, flourish even, fool everyone including her husband because she had her son to think of.

The walls of the room are coming in on me and I must get out of this chair.

"I apologise but I'm not feeling well. I would be grateful if I could use your bathroom," I say, jumping up from my seat.

"Of course. Follow me."

I climb the stairs with some urgency behind Susanna and she opens the door for me to enter then closes it quietly behind her. I listen to the sound of her footsteps ebbing away as she returns downstairs. I sit in the tiny room to wait for the tears. I wait to wring out the long-held anxiety, the regret, the tension, the disbelief now at Susanna's confession.

But for some reason the tears elude me. Perhaps the shock has taken over all other emotion for the time being.

Edward duped me so easily. I've discovered so much about him in such a short amount of time, including the fact it wasn't only me who brought out his dark side. The only saving grace is Daniel has been spared it.

Breathing heavily, I pull the neck of my dress. Oh, how I need to get out of this house, but I don't want to go home. I'm trapped, panicked, and feel faint as I have nowhere to run. I dash to the sink and run cold water over my wrists to calm me and slowly my breathing returns to normal.

Eventually, I've settled myself enough to return downstairs and face Susanna once more. I walk trance-like, my legs unsteady and, back in the hallway, I fight the urge to continue towards the door and out of the house. I'd rather not return to the oppression of the front room, but I must. I remember time is getting on, so Daniel's school day will be over before too long and this will thankfully bring an end to this encounter.

She's staring at the empty grate when I walk in. The silence, only broken by the ticking of the mantle clock, unnerves me and I remain still, uncertain what to do or say. A glass of water is waiting by my chair. The small act of kindness touches me.

Lifting her head to look my way her expression is kinder, almost compassionate. I bask in it a second but then I see her eyes travel down from my face to my stomach. They fly back up again, and I see the slight drop of her lower lip as I notice too late my coat has come undone.

"You're having a child," she gasps, almost falling into her chair.

Flustered, I fasten my buttons hastily. I watch her digesting the magnitude of the discovery, her expressions changing with each passing thought. I hold fast to the back of the settee to steady myself because I haven't been invited to sit.

She looks at me in a daze.

"Is the child your husband's?" she asks, the light from the window opposite making the tears sparkle in her eyes.

A hot flush rises from my chest to my cheeks.

"Yes," I say, hurriedly, "I know this will be little consolation but by my honour we only ever shared one kiss before you were married. It was the moment of weakness which began this sorry tale."

She breathes loudly through her nose and closes her eyes a second or two.

"I have no right I know, but I ask for your discretion," I say now.

Inside I'm pleading, my heart pounding as she continues to stare at me. She hangs her head then dabs her eyes with a crisp white handkerchief she pulls from the pocket of her dress.

"Please, Susanna, I implore you. I haven't told Freddie yet as I wanted to be sure."

Did I see a glimpse of concern cross her face?

"I don't understand what you mean," she says.

"I'm terrified the distress will affect the pregnancy and I can't disappoint him after all the years we've tried for a baby. You might think me silly, but I don't want to tempt fate."

She blows out a huge breath now saying, "What a fine mess we're both in, Effie. One kiss has brought about all this drama, all this trauma."

I realise my future is now entirely in the hands of a woman who owes me nothing.

"What on earth are you going to do?" she asks, finally, "I mean, if Freddie should be sent to prison."

I can't make plans as they would be so out of reach right now.

"I'm trying to take one day at a time, but it's difficult when the future is so uncertain. My mother is fading daily, and I can only watch on and wait. My life is out of my hands at the moment, so I'm unable to make any definite plans."

A strand of hair comes loose as she wipes her hand across her brow, and she no longer looks the epitome of elegance. So much has changed since I walked into this house.

"You must tell him, Effie, and soon. If I've noticed, then surely others will, including Freddie. This is good news, and good news is what both of you need now. You must trust all will be well with the baby."

"I didn't come here to add to your worries, only to apologise. When my mother passes, I intend to sell the hall and leave the village. You won't have to watch me living close by as a daily reminder."

She nods to the settee, and I sit down gladly.

"Perhaps I need the reminder of what I did. I realise now I'm not entirely without fault because once I was rid of Edward from the house every night, I could keep all I had and enjoy it. I used how he felt about you to my own advantage and in many ways, I was the real winner in this situation."

I'm still astounded at the high price she was willing to pay for her son.

"When he told me he was leaving me that night, it hit me that I hated him but also needed him in equal measure. I panicked at the thought of losing all the benefits which came with being Mrs Edward Cooper, the village schoolmaster's wife, and I was afraid for Daniel's future. I wanted to run after Edward, but instead I sat tight hoping you would refuse to leave Freddie. I couldn't lose face. I wish now I'd gone after him, if only to stop the terrible repercussions of the encounter."

She dabs her nose and I wonder how many times she's cried over her husband. I want to ask if she's relieved that he's run away but I don't.

"I know one thing however, Effie, and it will be cold comfort. In his own dark, twisted way Edward loved you. He loved you just as much as I imagine Freddie loves you, except Edward's was a nasty, jealous love. I know it because I knew him. Nothing is black and white, Effie, nothing. You must understand for your own state of mind. If you can't do it for yourself, then you must think about your unborn child's welfare."

I stifle a sob, a strange noise escaping me.

"Let it out, for your own good, let it out," she says as I sit with my head in my hands.

"I mustn't," I whisper, "if I start, I shall never be able to stop, but I need you to know the truth. We weren't together every night. Edward watched the house, and I finally went out to see him to ask him to stop hounding me. I was upset as Janet had just told me she was pregnant; Freddie was never home we were still expecting our problems to disappear overnight, living in false hope of a miracle. Janet's news left me reeling. I was confused and vulnerable, or I might not have gone outside to challenge him."

I pause and take a welcome sip of water. The next part will be the hardest, but she must know, I owe her the explanation.

"The final time was when I asked him to meet me at the brewery. I was desperate by then; I told him he must leave me alone and be with his family or I would disclose where he went each night. I didn't know the man he was … the man he is then."

I close my eyes to the recollection.

"That meeting did not … go to plan at all. That was when…" I stop mid-sentence when her raised hand indicates that I don't need to go any further.

"I know," she says, "I saw the state of you on your return to the village. You'd tidied yourself up, but the trauma was etched all over your face. I was paying far more attention than either of you realised."

I jolt my head up to look at her, a knowing smile about her lips making her appear far too mature for her years—she can't be thirty yet. She tucks the errant hair behind her ear, so she looks composed and the one in control of the situation again.

"How long was it before Edward returned home?" I ask.

She raises her eyes to recall.

"About an hour later, I think."

"You know I had to take drastic measures to escape. I thought for a moment I might have killed him when I lashed out at him, but I knew he was alive as I could hear him yelling my name as I mounted my bicycle."

"Good lord, Effie, you were lucky … and brave. I know he can turn so quickly and when you least expect it. I doubt I would have been as quick-thinking, though I've had a near miss or two myself."

"We all surprise ourselves sometimes," I say.

We share a small smile.

"Now though, your next step is telling Freddie about the baby. You owe him that and a baby will be a welcome new focus."

I nod. She's right, I've done all I can do for the time being to try to make amends, so now is the time."

She suddenly looks at the clock on the mantle remembering something I'd forgotten.

"I'm sorry but I must collect Daniel from school shortly. I'll walk back to the hall with you if you'll wait for me a moment."

Bustling past me, she goes into the hallway to put on a light jacket and the sad black hat I've seen her walk past the hall in of late. I'm calmer and glad to be having her companionship for the short journey home.

I think of how to tell Freddie about the baby. I only hope I'm not premature in giving him a new focus for the future.

She slams the front door shut and we stand side by side on the pathway. I imagine the faces peering out of the windows, the faces hidden away yet carefully positioned behind the curtains to get the best view. We'll be the talk of the village tomorrow, but how odd to think they will be none the wiser about our new connection.

Other than our sombre attire we look like any pair of friends taking a stroll in the sunshine, stepping in time, bags over our arms. If only they knew the half of it.

"I think I'll tell him straight away," I say suddenly.

"Yes, I think it would be wise to strike while the iron's hot. You found the strength to come and see me so you should consider yourself invincible now."

Still walking, we look at each other as we approach the iron gates of the hall, united in more than one secret. We don't exchange farewell greetings I think because we both instinctively know this won't be the last time. I only incline my head before entering and Susanna does the same. I watch her continue her short journey to collect her son from school.

As I approach the house along the gravel drive, I stand still wanting to stall for time. I'm at risk of losing momentum and the courage I had only seconds ago with Susanna by my side. Weary, I lean against the cover of the old yew tree. I must at least take a breath.

I gaze at the beautiful hall, its mullioned windows twinkling like eyes in the afternoon sunshine. How lucky I've been to live here all my life and I understand why my mother refuses to leave. I picture her in the attic, clinging to a life no longer worth living. But I will always admire her almost indefatigable spirit.

Betty has moved in for this short period to provide care for my mother around the clock out of the goodness of her heart and her love for me. I intend to reward her when our financial affairs are in order, though we could never repay the debt with money alone.

Freddie's bike is leaning against the garage door. I can't hide any longer. The moment has arrived to tell him my secret come what may.

My mouth is dry as I close the heavy door behind me then head to the dresser at the bottom of the stairs to remove my hat, cotton gloves and jacket. I adjust my blouse slightly to restore my disguise, then tidy my hair in the mirror before turning to head towards the stairs. All is quiet down here so Freddie must be in our room.

I look up to begin my ascent just as Freddie appears at the top of the stairs. His smile tells me he's pleased to see me.

"Hello, my love," I say, returning his smile, "please can you come downstairs a moment, I have a surprise for you."

Chapter 25

The light outside the cottage is changing, the blackness filtering to the hazy inkiness of dawn.

Is it my imagination or are her eyes set deeper than when we began our conversation, her face more sunken? This has been the longest night, yet tiredness is not what fades her. The fire is low but neither of us are cold, our minds too busy to be concerned with such prosaic sensations as fatigue and coldness.

"The pain you are living with was startling, obvious from the first time I laid eyes on you. It disturbs me still," the old woman says.

"I have no idea what to do with myself," I say, "I can't allow myself to break, for the sake of people who love me, for my baby most of all. But it would be sweet relief from the torment if I could. You and your cottage have been welcoming this past week; absorbing myself in your world has given me reprieve from my own. I don't want to go back."

I look into her eyes, the stain only visible in my peripheral vision now and soon it will be gone, I can sense it. I care deeply for this face, and it would be wrong to see it without the stain now.

"My dear, I'm old but I do not profess to be wise of the world outside this woodland. I've been locked away in here for so long, but I know without doubt you must face the truth. You must face it so you're not stuck in this quandary, and you must face it now. It will be too late otherwise for the people waiting and living in hope of seeing you again."

Wrapping my arms around my stomach I hold tight to my baby and hope the people she mentions are still part of my world. I would gladly give my soul to change the path I've chosen to lead me here tonight.

Suddenly she straightens her back and quickly moves to the edge of her seat as though ready to pounce. Her pain, and fragility have disappeared, and I turn my astonished face towards her. As I sit frozen in my chair, I'm unable to predict what could be about to unfold.

"Listen very carefully, I implore you. Now is the time, now or it will never be time, you know it, as do I. Listen to what I'm telling you before we miss an opportunity which can never come again."

Layer upon layer of anxiety rises within me, leaving me with a sharp pain in my chest. It takes my breath. My child moves urgently, somehow aware of the gravitas of the situation. Yet I have no clue what this could be.

In the depths of her eyes, I see plainly what she has unveiled. The translation is complete, and I slowly begin to understand. My tears are brimming, ready to fall. I know I must do as she asks, or these tears will entomb me, never to see the light of day again.

"I don't know where to begin!"

The words burst out from my mouth in almost a yell.

"You do," she says, her voice quieter yet still firm, insistent, "I'm here. I'm waiting to hear what you need to tell me, what you must tell me."

She sits back and closes her eyes. I stare at her, my panic subsiding slowly and her calmness allows me to process my thoughts and start to feel again. I've almost regained composure, at least enough to say the words she wants to hear in this new reality, a reality I now face with someone who knows they must be cruel to be kind.

"I understand now you're referring to the fact I haven't told you the truth. Although not a lie, I haven't been honest with myself," I pause, "at least, not entirely."

My tone is steady. She remains perfectly quiet and still, waiting patiently until I'm finally ready to complete this act of contrition.

She may be a witch. Not the broomstick and cauldron witch of the fairy tales; no, a sage, a soother, a teller of truths even when you don't want to hear them and I know with complete certainty now that I never want to leave her, leave this cottage, this woodland refuge. I wonder if I have a choice, but I will soon know the answer.

"I have found it impossible to admit to the ending of our story. I've played with the facts to make them more tolerable if they ever could be. I've always been mindful to think of the story in a way which subdues the havoc I created and the wider consequences.

But the truth is the only thing which will sever the shackles of my mind. You began that process tonight when you showed me the mark on your face. There is no more time left."

I'm resigned to telling my tale; a tale she already knows.

"I need to rid myself of the lies I've told myself in order to survive; lies which are grinding away at me day after day, breaking my mind and spirit.

*

"Some of what I've told you is the truth. I did leave Susanna that day and continue up the path to Carleton Hall to confess to Freddie he was going to be a father, that we were finally to become parents.

I did force myself to brush aside thoughts of a future without him if he should go to prison. I knew we would survive it. I knew it because we loved each other unconditionally and had reached a different level of understanding. There was only ever one girl for Freddie, one girl he carried in his heart. He took the blame for what happened during our marriage and laid it at his own door. He craved forgiveness. To my mind it was six of one and half a dozen of the other—we had both made mistakes and I told him so when we spoke of it.

Our next chapter as a family would give him hope for the future, something on the horizon. A life without hope is no life.

Susanna's eyes were upon me as I walked up the drive then I disappeared around the rear of the house to enter via the kitchen as I usually did. I glanced upwards and imagined my mother laying in the attic. I *was* grateful to have such a home, thankful she too had such a home. All this is my truth.

The next image flashes and stays in my mind, making me hold fast to my cheeks with each hand in distress. I draw a huge breath from the pit of my stomach as though preparing to jump into a blazing fire to rescue someone.

"The house was unnervingly quiet but for the same birdsong as the day my mother confided in me. I was immediately unsettled by it.

Had Freddie found out about the baby I wondered, but how could he have done? I was afraid, my fear cold and irrational.

As I pushed the kitchen door open, there was a strong peculiar smell; so powerful I instinctively put my hand over my nose and mouth. The rear of the house was always darker than the front from the shadow cast by an ancient beech tree so, as I always did, I switched on the light as I entered.

One small, insignificant act in a world of chaos and torment. A roar filled my ears, so loud it could surely have woken the dead. Simultaneously, a hurricane wind rushed through the doorway catapulting me off my feet and into the air."

I pause and see the old woman still sitting with eyes closed. The movement of the bone at the side of her ear, clenching and unclenching her jaw, is a sign of distress as she listens to my tale. I put my head in my hands again sensing the pain I am inflicting, but I'm bound now to my course to the very end.

"Whether it be a curse or a blessing, I remember nothing more of that moment. I only know what transpired from snippets of information pieced together from the accounts of others.

I awoke in a strange environment. I'd no clue as to what had happened and why I should be there. More confused than fearful at that point, it took a few minutes to realise I was in a hospital bed. But how, when only seconds before to my mind, I had been entering the kitchen at Carleton Hall?

"Ah, my dear," a stranger said to me, "You're back with us at last. My name is Mr Fieldhead, I am a consultant here at St. Mary's; I'm so very pleased to make your acquaintance finally."

Staring at him then I forgot his name and the name of the hospital immediately.

"I'm sorry. I know you must be confused but there's plenty of time to catch up."

His elderly face was pleasant, and I so wanted his reassuring smile to give me comfort.

It was as though I'd stepped out of a tunnel. I was blinking madly at the harsh lighting above my bed, so he leant forward to switch it off. My mouth was bone dry, my tongue cracked and swollen. A nurse in a pristine uniform stepped from behind him to pass me a tumbler of water.

"Sip, Delfina, but please don't overdo," she said kindly.

I took many sips then lay back on the pillow, wondering exactly how long I had been in a hospital.

I suddenly had a flashback of going into the kitchen of Carleton Hall and in pure terror at the recollection, I instinctively reached for my stomach. Mr Fieldhead smiled knowingly then and nodded. My baby had survived. The relief engulfed me, but then I tried to sit up. I wanted answers to many other questions—about Freddie, my mother, Betty, but mainly Freddie.

"What about Freddie, my…" I began my list.

The doctor shook his head.

"All in good time. You mustn't tire yourself. I need to do some tests first and then we can talk later."

"Today?" I asked quickly.

"Yes, today but now you're awake, you understand I must make your baby my priority."

There was nothing more I could say for the time being, but I was unable to comprehend how I could be so tired when I'd obviously been sleeping for some time. I know now I was full of sedative and painkillers and couldn't stay conscious even though I wanted to. Each time I awoke it was only for a short time and mostly the room was empty. If a nurse was in the room, she skilfully distracted me from any meaningful conversation.

I'm not certain how long I was left like that. Time loses meaning in such circumstances, I never asked because in the end it wasn't important.

The old woman's eyes remain closed. I take a swig of cold tea and stare into the dead grate.

"After a few days, the doctor reduced my painkillers, but not so much that I had complete awareness.

With my body healing it was apparent that I couldn't stay in hospital forever and a date was set for me to leave. I had no foothold, nothing solid to cling to, only a knot of apprehension that I was not going to like my new life whatever it may turn out to be.

That day unfamiliar footsteps accompanied the steady tread of Mr Fieldhead heading down the corridor. I knew his tread well by then. You take in the smallest most unimportant observations I think when you've nothing else to do. The absence of clocks meant I'd no idea if it was morning or afternoon but decided on morning as I'd had some food, washed, and dressed myself, then settled in a chair by the window. I was wearing a crumpled beige skirt, a white blouse, and some fur-lined house shoes, but they were too big to be my own and not a style I would have chosen. So much unfamiliarity.

I'd decided if they didn't discharge me that day, I would be discharging myself. If I didn't find out the answers, I thought I might go mad if I wasn't already.

Mr Fieldhead appeared in the open doorway, but I knew without him telling me there was somebody else with him, waiting out of sight. I hoped then it was Betty. I so wanted it to be Betty so she could settle me with her pragmatic words of wisdom.

"Well now, I think you've recovered sufficiently enough to have a little chat," Mr Fieldhead said, crouching, so we were at eye-level, "I'm sure you're keen to know more about why you are here. We thought it best to arrange for your friend to talk to you. I'm sorry for the delay, Delfina, I know it will have been difficult, but it was entirely necessary, I assure you."

"Thank you," I say weakly, thinking I could be sick, "I'd be grateful for the delay to come to an end now as quickly as possible, I'm afraid my politeness is wearing thin somewhat."

He reached to gently pat my hand. If it wasn't Betty only inches away, I could only hope the person waiting to speak to me might be Janet; that she'd taken pity on me and my situation. What is my situation exactly I wondered, surely fear of the unknown is greater than reality however harsh.

Mr Fieldhead turned and headed from the room, nodding once to the anonymous person.

For a moment they were silhouetted by the hall lights but as they approached, they came into focus. I was then face to face with the last person on earth I would have expected to be waiting to speak to me as a friend:

Susanna.

Chapter 26

Birdsong startles me in the silence of the cottage.

It has become a trigger to rekindle memories, such an evocative trigger, a reminder of days gone by and long ago, another life. I have an increasing sense of urgency. The night is nearly over, and I must finish my story once and for all. I know this, as she knows too.

"That day Susanna was looking at me differently, her expression one of pity. I'm sure I must have looked a pathetic sight with the ill-fitting clothes hanging from my thin frame.

Good manners made me want to get up from my chair, but she put her hand gently on my shoulder to stop me. I remember I was thankful as the effort was making the room swim.

"Stay where you are, dear," she said quietly, "as the doctor explained, I come here today as a friend."

I tried to line my thoughts up in some semblance of order, but when I did a cold hand took a firm grip of my heart. If Susanna was here, where was Freddie, where was Betty, Janet? The behaviour of the staff, Susanna's expression, they were only confirming my new life would be far from the life I'd had before.

She rushed to grab a chair and place it opposite me, taking my hands. I knew she was seeking to ease my unknown pain. I stared down at our locked hands then back into her eyes.

"What is it, Susanna? Please just tell me. The medication, sedation, whatever they've given me, is wearing off. I just need to know quickly … please."

She was holding so tightly to my hands she was hurting them, but I couldn't tell her. Shuffling in her seat, she looked out of her depth.

"Oh Effie, you must brace yourself," she said, then whispered to herself it seemed: "Where to start?"

She gripped my hands even tighter.

"Freddie has also been injured. I'm so sorry I must come here with bad news when you're so fragile."

I was strangely relieved for a second or two; she didn't say, "Freddie is dead", or "Freddie has died," and that was what I was expecting I realised. However, I soon moved along to understanding Freddie must be in a bad way or he would have come to see me.

I knew by the look on her face and the constant movement of her lips, there was more. She was grappling with her words.

"You must take me to him. How badly is he injured? Please be truthful, Susanna, I don't wish to waste any more time."

"He's been unconscious since the accident like you, but the doctors are worried. He isn't doing well at the moment but thankfully he was far enough away to not bear the brunt of the blast only the debris."

Tears were in her eyes, and I thought of that day I gathered the courage to see her at her home. The day everything was revealed. She told me I should consider myself invincible after facing her. I would have to find the courage yet again.

"I must go to him. When he sees me, he'll get better, I know it."

"I'll take you, I promise," she said, "but only once the doctor has assured me you are well enough."

The strange smell in the house, an explosion. It was all becoming clear, all too clear.

"My mother?" I asked, panic rising.

"I'm afraid your mother was too ill, Effie. The doctors say she would have died within hours, regardless. She knew nothing."

My mother gone. It wasn't true surely, it couldn't be. My thoughts carried on turning, turning.

"What about Betty?" I asked frantically.

Relief wafted fleetingly behind her eyes.

"Thankfully Betty is unhurt, she'd left the hall to walk to the chemist for your mother's medication."

I was so grateful for a moment, but then my mind replayed the stark reality over and over. It was too much to contemplate but I couldn't make it stop. Freddie is seriously ill, my mother gone.

I pictured Susanna lying awake, preparing for this moment. I thought of her imagining every scenario of how this conversation might unfold, every reaction I might have.

"Please, Effie, listen very carefully to what I have to say," she raised my chin then with a forefinger to be sure she had my complete attention, "I know you will hold yourself responsible, but you mustn't. The police have already said they think it was a faulty connection to the oven which had caused a build-up of gas. It could have happened at any time to anyone. How could you have known? Whatever you do, please don't see this as part of the chain of events when it's entirely separate."

I wanted to dare to believe her words of comfort.

As I got up slowly from my chair to shuffle and stand by the window, I watched the comings and goings of the hospital grounds as though everything was normal, nothing had changed.

All I had was the stark numbness of nothingness. I should have been wailing, dropping to my knees, and sobbing my heart dry. But it was all too great to process in my mind. I felt anaesthetised, dead within.

"Why didn't Betty come today?" I asked Susanna then, immediately realising it sounded as though I wished it had been Betty and not her. "I apologise, I only mean Betty was the obvious choice."

"She's had many practicalities to deal with. She was set to come, but I offered because I'm an outsider, whereas Betty is in the thick of the situation. She loves you. I wanted to spare her the pain of delivering such terrible news. I wanted to help."

At the mention of Betty, I thought of Carleton Hall, our home such as it was. I wondered if it was still standing and asked the question. I could see Susanna in the reflection of the window, raising her head to look my way.

"I'm sorry to say the hall suffered significant damage in the blast. I don't know whether it can be saved but this problem can wait for now," she said, "Betty has offered you her cottage as your home for as long as you wish. Her mother extends the same invitation."

I closed my eyes, reflecting briefly on all I owed Betty for her years of unwavering loyalty and devotion. I wondered then how I could repay her when I had nothing.

Susanna had taken up the poisoned chalice.

"You really drew the short straw in coming here today, Susanna and I will always be grateful to you for the gesture."

It was impossible to read her expression, so I could never have predicted what she would say to me then. It was only later I understood how profound her words were.

"We are bound, Effie, you and I. Bound by the truth. We can be friends and I promise you can lean on me. We must hold fast to each other as only you and I know the whole of the matter. You need me now, but I also need you in my own way because only you understand. Remember this when the facts are playing with your mind. You made one small mistake but afterwards you always tried to do the right thing. You are a good person."

A good person, a good person, a …

"I'm going to find the doctor, but I'll be back as quickly as possible. I know you're desperate to see Freddie."

A good person, a good person, a …

I was conflicted by the bitter sweetness of her words, though there was no questioning their sincerity.

Outside the world went on its weary way. An unknown person rushed in the rain towards the entrance of the hospital, a car set off towards the gates, but I was miles and miles away from the scene outside and the scene within that room.

I'd lost my place in the world.

Alongside my mother, my home, God forbid my husband …

I too was gone.

Chapter 27

It's time for me to leave.

I stand now ready to make a move. The old woman opens her red eyes wide, startled by my sudden movement.

"Stop, sit down, you are still not ready!"

She doesn't raise her head from the back of the chair, but her voice is commanding. I step back and perch on the edge of my seat. Much like my mother, you cannot pull the wool over this woman's eyes.

She rolls her eyes in my direction without lifting her head.

"I know what you want from me, I understand only too well," I tell her.

After baring my soul this long night, I'm too exhausted to take the final step. I'm hesitating because of the distress it will cause—I already want to flee from the cottage.

"I cannot. It is too much, surely you must know," I plead.

Her eyes narrow with the first true sign of disapproval, forcing me to look away.

"Then this whole night will have been for nothing," she says.

This time I see a desolation in her eyes. I must not turn away; I must face it.

I'm shivering, the fire long since died, the blue light of a snowy dawn stealing the warmth from the once cosy room. Time is ebbing away, I must end this for her sake, and mine.

I rise from my chair, towering over her. I quietly remove my black woollen scarf, letting it drape across my shoulders to finally reveal the truth that she has doggedly coaxed out of me; the truth that binds us together for all time. I am not brave, I am not strong, but I must let her see her heart's desire.

A single sob escapes her. I drop to my knees, burying my head in her lap, pushing my face deeper and deeper into her skirts. I hear wailing, like ensnared animals, trapped without a hope of escape. Surely such a sound cannot be coming from us. Yet there is no one to hear us or save us.

"You are right, Effie. Tell me; tell me the whole of it," I plead.

I pull my face from the security of her lap, but my head remains bowed, in deference. I defer to her, to her wisdom.

She strokes the top of my head but nothing she does will give me comfort until she speaks the truth.

Until she speaks our secret out loud.

"We have been in hiding from this world and the shame of the past for too long. The shame that has marked us for life so we could never truly find happiness. You must let go of the shame before we can face the next part of our journey. If Freddie lives or dies, we must face what comes head on for the sake of our baby.

You must draw strength from somewhere before we can resume our life, healed in both mind *and* spirit to find peace to go on."

The wind gusts and rattles the outer door. It is suddenly flung open and there on the doorstep is Susanna, her distraught face reddened from the bitter cold, drifting snow engulfing her boots.

Reality gushes in like a tidal wave; images of the past, the present and an untold future mingling as one.

Susanna has been true to her word and is the one who's supported me to live this life of chosen solitude in the old groundsman's cottage, the hall long since demolished.

I could not have done it without her. She threw me a lifeline when I needed it most and our bond has been steadfast.

I'm startled as she rushes towards me now.

"Effie," she says, her gentle voice melting me, soothing me just the same as it always has, "I'm so glad I got here in time. Something told me to come, I sensed you were in far more pain than you said. You forget I know you too well, though you try to hide it from me."

"This is my friend Effie," I whisper, "I came to talk to her, to tell her my story. It was time."

Susanna does not acknowledge our guest. Instead, she holds onto my shoulders, fixing me with a steely gaze to command my attention.

"Now just you get a hold of yourself, Delfina Braithwaite-Walker if you will. Let me tell you what I must tell you as I've thought of so little else these weeks. I should be considered an authority.

Forgive yourself as I have forgiven you.

Edward is the one to blame.

He lost his mind after he lured you into a relationship when you were little more than a child. He did not know; you did not know then how deep his twisted love was running.

I know Freddie's refusal to confront your difficulty conceiving left you frustrated, lonely and vulnerable. And we would be wise not forget that I was only too happy for long enough to allow this to happen for my own selfish reasons. This is a regret of my own, but we are not to blame."

Susanna's eyes are frantic and full of tears above her flushed cheeks, but she goes on trying to convince me that I am not the only person who should carry the blame.

"Listen to what I'm saying to you. Freddie protected you from harm as any husband would and what happened afterwards was out of your control. Perhaps Freddie went too far; but he is a good man who was pushed to the limit. The pain, the regret, you are drowning in it. Stop, I tell you, stop this minute!"

She drops her head and falls silent, panting, waiting. All the time she was speaking I was looking straight through her as though she wasn't there. She needn't have come, but she did.

The Truth.

Somewhere deep, deep inside me I hear it echo, faintly at first but growing louder, as if desperately seeking the surface, the light.

The Truth is what this night has all been for. It was hiding in plain sight all the time I think as I turn from Susanna to look deep into the old woman's eyes and the loving countenance of my saviour. I study the stain on her cheek as her hand touches mine, and we smile.

We began this New Year's Eve as strangers, but we are now united, ready to face whatever may be, because the truth has not set us free, *we* have set each other free. We have reconciled and can leave together filled with a love and absolute peace.

I am her past and she, my future.

We are as one, joined and whole.

Chapter 28

"There you are, how relieved I am to have finally found you. I have news, Effie."

I jump up from the chair, my blanket clutched in my hands.

I've been looking for you since yesterday as Betty had no idea where you were, but this morning I spotted the smoke from the chimney.

What could she have come to tell me?

"What news, Susanna? I hope you haven't more bad news to relay," I say, "if you have, please just tell me now and get it over with."

Her smile startles me. I haven't seen a smile in so long, too long.

"Perhaps it might be better if I show you."

She nods over my shoulder, and I spin around, my jaw dropping.

There by the door is Freddie … my dear Freddie.

I let out a laugh which borders on hysterical. Freddie is smiling too albeit a shadow smile, like it's taking all his effort. I'm overwhelmed, only thinking my mind may be unstable.

"I'll make myself scarce," Susanna says, stepping towards me.

She takes both my hands in hers and presses her lips gently to my cheek as I close my eyes.

"Effie, we have much to discuss but for now I will leave you alone with your husband."

I nod and smile because already she has helped me so much more than she could ever know. Now is not the time to speak of it, if I ever do, I think as my eyes wander back of their own accord to Freddie.

She touches his arm as she opens the door to leave us.

The day is snowy but sunshine floods the entrance to the cottage. It looks like I imagine the gates to heaven, glowing and white. Susanna disappears into the woodland.

I'm alone with my husband but my mind is struggling to accept he really is here. He does look like Freddie only slightly thinner. He has combed his hair, but his cheeks are bristly and in need of a shave.

"I think you should be in bed," I say quietly.

His smile is too weak.

"Now why would I want to be in a hospital bed when I can be with my girl?"

He walks slowly towards me then touches my shoulder, so I sit back down in the chair. I'm struggling with the most basic of functions it seems, as though I'm not part of this world. His hand on my shoulder though feels real enough.

As Freddie sits in the chair opposite mine, I remember the old woman. I sense she is near, but I don't see her. Surely, she can't have ventured out in this weather.

I want to ask Freddie but I'm suddenly self-conscious, remembering to hide my cheek behind my palm. I don't want him to see me in such a state.

"When did you wake?" I ask.

"Early yesterday morning, and I left hospital last night against the doctor's orders and my own better judgement. I admit it was a little too soon, but I was so desperate to see you. Susanna and Betty said you had been visiting every day since you were discharged from hospital, so they couldn't understand where you had gone. I just couldn't wait to see you when I awoke."

I stare at the woollen blanket still in my hand. The old woman gave me this blanket to settle me, try to ease my torment.

"Freddie, I'm so sorry. I thought I'd lost you; I'd convinced myself of it. The regret … the regret was too much."

He bends to kneel on the floor, and I notice the fire I thought was dead is ablaze, the colours of the flames flickering my way in all their vibrant life.

"My love, I am real, I am here, you must believe it. The trauma, the loss has been too great, and I knew none of it, I couldn't help you. I am the one who is sorry."

His hand lay on mine, the warmth seeping into my heart so I start to believe.

"Prepare yourself," I say, "I must tell you what I wanted to tell you that awful day though it will be a shock, perhaps surprise is a better word," I take a deep breath as he looks on, brow furrowed, "Freddie, we are to be parents, finally you are to become a father."

His eyes grow wide then drop to my stomach. He stares so long at it then slowly holds out his hand to move the blanket. He traces the roundness with one finger then gently spreads his palm to feel it properly in his hand.

"No, it can't be, Effie. Now I don't know if this day is real. Please tell me it is real."

Smiling, I touch his dear face, pure elation etched in every crease. This man is so happy, and this in turn gives me untold happiness. He has waited for this moment, he deserves it.

"After I went to see Susanna, I went back to the hall to tell you the good news. She has been a true friend," I say.

His fingers still stroking my stomach gently, he's unable to move his eyes away.

"Indeed, she has been in more ways than you know," he says.

His eyes finally reach and hold mine.

"Susanna has been searching for Cooper. She came to tell you yesterday she had found him after following a lead from the headmaster at Loftus school. He wasn't far away after all, but she says he won't be bothering us again."

I search his face.

"I don't understand, what about the court case?"

He smiles: "Susanna's been busy on our behalf. Cooper has agreed to withdraw his statement and move away in exchange for Susanna agreeing to a divorce. Without it the police will have no option but to drop the charges," he adds, his eyes twinkling with that old sparkle I love so much.

I drop my head back and heave a great sigh. Thank God for my friend and her astuteness. She is a fine ally.

"This is surely the best start to a new year anyone could wish for, Freddie."

"We will be happy here as we were before all this. Do you remember how good life was living in our tiny cottage as newlyweds? It can be the same again and this time with our longed-for child."

I beam at my husband and run my finger over the greyness of his face. He must rest, it's too soon for him to be out of bed. I glance at the empty seat behind him.

My face drops as I remember the night.

"My mind was in turmoil Freddie. I've held onto untold guilt and shame for so long. I know you may think it strange, but I'm indebted to a friend who came when I had nowhere to turn. I was drawn here, and she was so wonderful and wise. She consoled me, made me believe I had the strength to go on come what may."

He shakes his head, uncertain to whom I'm referring. Perhaps it might have been best to keep my counsel even from Freddie. No matter, I see no reason to elaborate.

"It has been a long night, but all I know is that it wasn't my time to leave this world as it wasn't yours, my love," I say, "there is hope for happier days for us now, though sadly the stain will always be a reminder of past mistakes."

"Stain? What stain do you mean, Effie?" he asks.

I stare at him then close my eyes, slowly moving my hand from my face. His eyes drop to look at my cheek, his face devoid of any reaction whatsoever.

"The mark from the explosion," I say.

His hand goes to touch my cheek and I jerk my head away. He gets to his feet.

"My love, come stand with me a moment," he says holding out his hand.

When I don't move, he tries to take my hand to lift me from the chair, but I shake my head. I know what he wants me to do.

"No, Freddie, I can't, please don't make me."

I pull away from him as he reaches out again to touch my cheek. He drops his hand.

"My love, do you trust me?" he asks.

"Yes," I say without a second's hesitation. My trust in Freddie is absolute, it always has been I realise now. He stands by the mirror for so long I know he wants me to join him. I wait a moment wondering if I can.

Sighing, I accept I will one day have to look at what I don't want to see. That day may as well be today. I get up from my seat to stand by his side.

"Please, Effie, do as I ask, look and see what I see," he says.

I stand on tiptoes then close my eyes, taking a deep breath. I finally find the courage to open them to my reflection.

Staring at my face, my face stares back.

My complexion is just as it was before the accident aside from the merest hint of pinkness, too faint to notice without close inspection. How can it be? I run my fingers over my cheek, tiptoeing closer to the mirror to get a better view. Is the pinkness even there, I wonder or is it just another illusion I've created.

Freddie's face sits above mine in the reflection and he's studying me intently.

"Whatever happened to your face, my darling girl, you can be sure it has healed."

"I couldn't bear to look at my face, Freddie. I thought of the mark as a stain on me. It was a stain I thought I must live with forever as my punishment."

He bends to kiss my cheeks, my forehead then finally my lips. My eyes close and one tear slides down my cheek.

But the floodgates do not open. How could they open when gratitude is flowing so freely instead?

I am on my way to being healed, and not only by my husband and my friends but most importantly … by the only person who ever had the true power to mend me.

About the author

Jo Priestley is a Yorkshire author committed to writing historical fiction, based on real lives and real people. She grew up with tales by the fireside, poignantly told by her grandmother, in her crumbling but grand house on the outskirts of Leeds, England, creating the perfect atmosphere.

She has been a professional business writer all her career, and now she would like to share the fictional stories that have been waiting in the wings, until the time was right.

After almost ten years of writing, six novels were published in 2023, with her next book due to be published in June 2024. The books feature women who have their own tale of love, life and friendship to tell, and are set in and around Bronte Country. She is a proud member of the Society of Authors.

Jo considers the raising of five strong, kind-hearted daughters to adulthood her greatest achievement. Now she would like to commit herself as much to her passion for storytelling.

Printed in Great Britain
by Amazon

50612978R00158